THE AGENCY OF SUPERNATURAL EVENTS

The Agency of Supernatural Events

The Doctor

JUSTIN RICHMAN

Also By Justin Richman

The Defenders Saga:

1. The Silver Hood
2. Deathwish

The Agency of Supernatural Events: The Doctor
May, 2023
First Printing, 2023

This is a work of fiction. Names, characters, places and incidents either are the product of the author's imagination or are used fictitiously. Any resemblance to actual persons, living or dead, events or locales is entirely coincidental.

ISBN-979-8-9850601-6-4

Edited by Tim Major
Cover Design by Thea Magerand
www.ikaruna.eu/

| 1 |

The Doctor placed the black canister on the floor delicately, wary of what it contained—a virus of his own making. If it was somehow accidentally released into the atmosphere, his entire project would be jeopardized. How would he be able to continue his work?

This virus wasn't for him. It was for everyone else.

He had spent months researching it. Cultivating it. Analyzing it and perfecting it. And now he was going to test it out. Just one step closer to his ultimate creation.

This wasn't his end game, though. This was only the beginning.

The Doctor descended into the depths of his chosen hotel, feeling a chill emanating from every corner of its cold, concrete basement. With each step closer to what he deemed would be a groundbreaking experiment, anticipation churned inside him.

He unzipped a small black duffel bag and pulled out a screw-driver. He started unscrewing the vent attached to the wall. One by one, he withdrew the screws and set them aside. He pulled the grate off the wall and placed it gently on the ground.

The Doctor jumped as the door to the room he was in shut behind him. He turned to catch a glimpse of what had startled him.

"Hey! You there!" a voice called from behind him. "What are you doing?"

The Doctor took a deep breath, wishing he had been able to get through this setup without any disruptions. He was prepared for it, though. He rose and confronted the man approaching him.

"Hi there," the Doctor said. "I'm with maintenance. There was a problem with the ventilation. I should be out of here shortly."

The man wore a black suit and had nicely combed hair, brushed to the side. A name tag was pinned to his jacket—*Russell.* Attached to his belt was a walkie-talkie.

"Maintenance, huh? What's your name?" Russell asked.

"Tim," the Doctor replied.

Russell gave a friendly smile. "Hi, Tim. Problem is, I'm the general manager here and it would be entirely my responsibility to permit any maintenance work. Unfortunately, I haven't authorized any such work related to the ventilation of this building. So I'm going to ask again—what are you doing?"

It was a shame. The Doctor would have preferred Russell to become infected, to see how the virus affected him.

Oh well, he thought. *Just one less person to infect.*

"I told you, I'm working on the ventilation. Here," the Doctor added, "I'll show you the paperwork."

He reached into his coat pocket, withdrew a small handgun, aimed it at Russell and fired two shots. Russell had no time to react before being struck twice in the chest. He stumbled backwards and fell to the floor.

He'd have to hurry now. Someone else would surely have heard the gunshot.

The Doctor placed the handgun back inside his coat pocket and returned his attention to the vent. He bent down and lifted the black canister, placing it inside. He swiped his thumb at a small screen attached to the canister, which lit up in response to his touch. A timer blinked on the screen. He tapped the screen again. It beeped and began counting down from five minutes.

Quickly, he replaced the grate and secured the screws. He gathered his tools and zipped up his bag.

The Doctor rose, clutching his bag, and approached Russell lying on the floor. He was still alive, barely. Blood was dripping from his mouth. His breathing was labored. His jacket was soaked in his own blood. It wouldn't be long now.

The Doctor smiled at Russell—the same friendly smile Russell had offered moments before.

The Doctor left the room and headed for the nearest exit from the hotel.

He couldn't wait to see the damage his virus would create. He wanted to watch people suffer. He needed to learn from it and perfect it much more.

Everyone in the hotel would soon be infected.

| 2 |

Four hours later...

Flashing red and blue lights brightened the dimly lit streets this evening. Police cars surrounded the Pavilion Hotel. Every door was barricaded, preventing anyone from entering or exiting the building.

A black SUV swerved around the corner and came to a screeching halt alongside a line of police cars blocking the street. All four doors of the vehicle opened and four people stepped out.

A man walked towards the barricade, followed by a woman and two younger men.

"Excuse me! Hold on!" a police officer said, trying to block them from going any further. "Where do you think you're going?"

Chris Hoffman pulled a badge from his pocket. "We're with TASE. There was a call about a pathogen in this hotel. We've been tracking the man responsible."

The officer cocked his head to the side and narrowed his eyes. "You're with... who?"

"The Agency of Supernatural Events," Chris said.

The officer still held his confused look. "Never heard of it."

Chris turned his attention to the hotel. "We're kind of new."

Chris Hoffman was the leader of an elite team known as The Agency of Supernatural Events. Though his short, gray hair hinted at years beyond many of the team, Chris kept himself in exceptional physical shape, making it difficult to guess he was 57 years old.

Jade Burleigh, Frank Parker, and Myles Johnson rounded out the rest of Chris's team.

Chris had been searching for an heir to lead the team when he retired, which is where Jade came in. Her tough-as-nails attitude—which was what had initially attracted Chris to her—suggested she would be more than up for the challenge. She was brunette, with green eyes and a fit, attractive physique, but it was her strength of character that made him sure of his choice—even at a young age of 29.

When he had reviewed her stats, she was always number one in physical training amongst her peers.

As soon as Chris had seen Jade's impressive academic record, he had known she was the one—a young woman with brains and brawn. He didn't hesitate to recruit her for his newly established team; having someone like Jade on board would be an invaluable asset.

Frank, on the other hand, was a loner. His buzzed head and scruffy beard made him look a little intimidating. Frank was an amazing shot with any firearm. He always liked to "lone wolf" any situation, rather than working with a team. You'd think that would be the opposite of what Chris would have wanted, but, in fact, it was perfect.

Frank was the wild card on the team—the unpredictable aspect. Chris didn't *truly* want unpredictability, but someone like Frank was capable of thinking outside the box.

Finally, there was Myles. Chris had found Myles after he graduated from the top of his class at a local college. The guy was a hacking and technology genius.

Chris had discovered his underground persona. Myles went by the hacker name Th3B1naryBand1t. Chris had confronted him with this information, calling him out on his hacking ability.

Problem was, Myles became overwhelmed in the face of danger. When Chris threatened him with what he knew of his illegal hacking activities, Myles buckled and joined the team rather than face the consequences.

The Agency of Supernatural Events was newly established. Its members had only performed a few missions together.

Their first had involved investigating a bus of passengers who had spontaneously combusted. When they had first arrived on the scene, the team had assumed it was just a bus accident, since it had crashed into a building. But when they stepped onto the bus and saw small body parts lying in piles of ash, they knew it was something different.

The team eventually located the terrorist behind the attack a few days later. He had used a chemical compound he released on the bus that melted its victims from the inside out once ingested.

The agency's second mission together was an investigation into a monster in the woods of Meyerstown. For about two months there had been reports about a giant monster. Two hunters had searched for it and had gone missing for three days. One of them returned finally, battered and haggard after his ordeal. The other hunter had disappeared without a trace. Despite how outrageous the survivor's story seemed, it didn't seem to resonate with the local law enforcement. He was considered a suspect in the other hunter's disappearance. Intrigued and concerned about what truly happened out there, Chris and his team had investigated the incident to uncover what really hid in those woods.

The agency had interviewed the man who had claimed the monster was at least eight feet tall, furry, with three arms and two heads. This clearly fit the agency's definition of "supernatural." The team tore the area apart looking for this creature, and they eventually found it, dying in a cave tucked deep into the forest. It wasn't technically a monster, but a mutated bear. They weren't sure how it had survived for as long as it did. But whatever mutation it had was clearly catching up with it.

This current mission was their thirteenth.

Lucky number thirteen.

The agency had attempted to capture the Doctor once before, but unfortunately they hadn't been successful. However, they had succeeded in preventing his heinous plan of unleashing a deadly pathogen on an unsuspecting population.

This time, the Doctor had eluded them, and now he had released his virus.

Chris glanced at the officer's name tag. "Look, Officer Cohen—oh, you were the one I spoke with on the phone."

The young officer nodded.

"So the person responsible for this mess goes by the name, the Doctor," Chris said. "He usually wears a white lab coat. Short, messy brown hair. About six feet tall. Seen anyone resembling that description?"

Officer Cohen shook his head.

"Can you tell me who the commanding officer is?" Chris asked.

"I am."

Chris looked the officer up and down. He couldn't have been older than 25. "You look a little young to be in charge here."

Officer Cohen shrugged his shoulders. "It's a small town. The chief, Larry—sorry, Officer Simmons, is on vacation in mountains this weekend. So I'm in charge for now. It's usually a quiet town. Nothing like this"—he gestured to the hotel—"happens around here.

Most of what we get are noise complaints, a few drunken idiots from time to time, and maybe breaking up an argument here and there."

Chris glanced at the hotel again. "You going to be able to handle this?"

The kid looked nervous. The shaking of his voice was a dead giveaway.

Officer Cohen nodded.

"Good," Chris said. "We need all hands on deck for this one. Make sure all the officers on your force are here."

Chris scanned the area and noticed two blankets laid out on the sidewalk in front of the hotel. There were two more in the street.

"Are these the bodies we spoke about when you called this in?" Chris asked.

"Yes. When we first arrived after getting a call about the shooting inside the hotel, myself and Officer Flynn were about to go inside to investigate. Two people came stumbling outside and rushed at us. At first we thought they were running from something in a panic. It wasn't until they got closer that we saw it."

"Saw what?" Chris asked.

Officer Cohen shook his head and sighed. "Their faces. They were full of rage. They were screaming—no, *growling*—as they ran towards us. They had these snarls on their face. When they were close, you could see the spit flying from their mouths. One had some kind of pipe in his hand. The other was unarmed. They both ran at full speed towards us. Like I said before, we thought they were running from something. But..." He trailed off.

"You had to shoot them," Chris said, nodding at the blankets on the street that covered the bodies.

"We had no choice!" His voice became higher and nervous. "One of them swung that pipe at Flynn. They attacked us. We told them to stop or we'd shoot. We warned them multiple times."

Chris put a hand on the kid's shoulder. "It's okay. You did what you had to do. It was them or you."

The young officer shook his head. "I didn't want to do it."

"I know you didn't."

Chris could tell the officer had never taken a life before. It was a tough thing to do, especially for someone as young as him. It was something he knew the officer would never forget.

"So, that tells me the story of those two bodies," Chris said, pointing to the two blankets in the street. "What about the two by the door?"

Officer Cohen sighed again. "Flynn and I wanted to go inside the hotel to see what was going on. We took one step into the lobby and two more people came rushing out of a room and sprinting down the hallway. It was like they were out to attack. I mean, if we hadn't gotten out of there, they probably would have tried to kill us."

"You left the building?"

"Yes. I didn't want to die. We ran and those people came running out after us. We shot them too. What's happening to those people in there? They aren't normal. I knew one of the people we killed. His name was Tom Neckerman. He was a butcher at our grocery store down the street," Officer Cohen said, pointing in another direction. "He was a good guy."

"I'm sure he was, and I'm sorry you had to do what you did. It was a difficult situation you found yourself in. But I need you to focus now, okay?"

The officer nodded.

"Good. Are all the doors sealed?"

"Yes. Myself and a few other officers locked everything after I spoke to you on the phone."

"Perfect. And no one has entered or exited the building?"

"Not to my knowledge. We were here moments after the call about the shooting. I mean, everything happened in such a short amount of time. But we had people watching all exits. I don't think anyone else has come out."

"Okay, good. Do you have the keys?"

Officer Cohen reached into his pocket and handed Chris a key ring with three keys on it.

"Thank you. I'm going to gather my team and head inside."

Chris walked away but Officer Cohen yelled after him, "You're going inside? With those crazies in there? They're going to kill you."

Chris smiled. He'd fought in worse situations over the years. A few people with rage problems didn't intimidate him.

He continued to walk away as he spoke. "My team and I will handle it. You just stay outside and watch the doors for us."

The young officer waved his hands in frustration and returned to his vehicle, stationed a few yards from the front door of the hotel. He stood by the passenger-side door and watched over the roof of the vehicle. The door to the hotel was locked.

A loud bang came from the front door.

Chris spun mid stride to face the door, feeling a collective stillness among his fellow teammates and the police officers. The noise startled Chris, making his heart rate rise. He stared intently, hoping the locked door would keep whatever was behind it at bay. With each passing moment, rising tension filled the air as they anxiously awaited to see what would happen next.

Suddenly, a series of loud bangs from inside the hotel broke the silence.

Chris hurried back to his team. They had to get inside. They had to figure out what was going on.

"Grab your suits and weapons," Chris told his team. "Get dressed. We're up."

| 3 |

As the team prepared themselves, the loud noises stopped. All eyes were focused intently on the door.

"Stevens is on his way to help analyze the pathogen," Jade said.

"Good. We'll go in and clear out a zone. We're in teams of two." Chris pointed at Frank. "You're taking lead. I don't want any of those raging lunatics to get to us. Got it?"

Frank nodded in agreement.

Chris continued. "Jade, stick with Frank. Myles," He turned to face him. "You're with me, covering our asses. Understood?"

Jade, Frank, and Myles answered simultaneously, "Understood."

"Alright, let's go."

Chris led his team through the swarm of police officers, wearing all-black hazmat suits. Each suit was encased in armor around the chest and stomach and had a black hood with an airtight face shield zipped around the neck for total protection. Attached at the back was a small but powerful box pumping clean oxygen into the outfit so they could breathe.

The suits contained all their tactical needs. Strapped around the waist was a utility belt with an extra magazine pouch on one leg and a handgun holster on the other. In their hands they each clutched an AR-15 with a shoulder strap.

One by one, the team lined up in front of the hotel door. Frank was in front. Jade stood to his right, followed by Myles and then Chris.

Chris used the keys he had received from Officer Cohen to unlock the front door.

He held up three fingers and counted down.

Three.

Two.

One.

As he pulled open the door, Frank moved inside immediately. Jade and Myles followed him. Chris made his way inside and shut the door behind him, locking it. He spun around and raised his gun.

The team froze in anticipation, weapons drawn and poised to fire at any target that might come their way.

Their eyes were immediately drawn to the grandeur of the two-story lobby. The polished wood panels behind a sleek front counter were illuminated by warm light from a fixture overhead.

The second floor of the lobby boasted an open lounge. A guard rail safely surrounded the area.

To their left was a cozy seating area containing tables and lounge chairs. A small bar was tucked in the corner. To their right, an empty hallway that led towards the hotel rooms.

The team scanned the lobby. It was quiet. There was no movement.

"Clear," Frank said.

Everyone lowered their weapons.

"Jade, find out how much longer until Stevens gets here," Chris said. "We need to know if the pathogen is still in the air and contagious."

Jade nodded, took her phone from her utility belt pouch, and started dialing.

Myles walked behind the front counter and began typing away at the computer.

"What are you doing?" Chris asked.

Myles kept his head down and continued typing even as he spoke. "I'm going through the list of guests the hotel has in its system. With it being almost evening, we'll probably have more than half of them in the building and needing to be accounted for."

"How many?" Frank asked.

"It looks like there are one hundred and seven people checked in. So—"

Frank interrupted. "Probably sixty or seventy then, right?"

"Possibly. There's really no way to make sure without going through and accounting for everyone. Oh!" Myles turned his attention to the computer again. "We also have the staff. I'm pulling up the employee list." He stopped typing and ran his finger down the screen. "Fourteen employees on for this evening."

"So, closer to eighty people inside the building?" Chris asked.

"It's an estimate. I don't know for sure. But if I had to guess, based on the time of day, yes," Myles said.

"Minus four," Frank said, referring to the four dead bodies outside.

Jade rejoined the group. "Stevens is about twenty minutes out."

"Good. Let's—" Chris began, but he stopped as a scream came from down the hallway.

All four team members raised their weapons and aimed towards the sound, then stood motionless, waiting.

Footsteps came from the hallway. Lots of them. It sounded like horses galloping.

"Hold. No one fire yet," Chris said.

The footsteps grew louder. They were getting closer. And fast.

"This is the police!" Chris shouted. "Come out with your hands raised or we will be forced to open fire."

The noises grew in intensity.

"I will only ask one more time," Chris said.

Someone came sprinting down the hallway at full speed. It was a man wearing jeans and a yellow T-shirt. He came charging at the team, growling and spewing spit from his mouth, as though he was rabid.

"Stop!" Frank yelled.

The man kept running. He was now only a few paces from the team.

Frank fired four shots. Every bullet struck the man in the torso. He fell flat on his face and slid to a halt by Frank's feet.

"Seventy-five to go," Frank said.

"Not cool, Frank," Jade said.

He shrugged. "What? It's true, isn't it?"

Suddenly, three more people came running from the hallway at full speed towards them, growling.

"We got company!" Jade said.

With guns blazing, they brought a swift end to the people approaching them. As quickly as the battle had started, it ended. With their guns still drawn, they waited tensely for anymore unexpected visitors to emerge. After several seconds had passed, they lowered their guns.

Jade stared at Frank. He smirked.

"Don't you say it," she said.

"Seventy-two," Frank said.

"You're an asshole," Jade replied, shaking her head and turning away.

"I know."

"Guys, focus," Chris said. "Frank may be an asshole, but he's got a point. A morbid one, though. We're looking for about seventy-two more people. Either we need to be prepared to fight and defend ourselves against them, or they may already be dead. We know nothing yet. But we have to be prepared."

"I'm prepared," Frank said, raising his weapon again.

"Guys," Jade said. "Come here."

Chris and Frank walked towards the hallway, and Myles left the counter to join them. They saw Jade kneeling by a body in the middle of the hallway.

"What do you have, Jade?" Chris asked.

"A body. Female," Jade replied. "Probably the scream we heard."

"Are they killing each other?" Myles asked.

Jade looked up at him and shrugged.

"Doubtful," Frank said. "The way the three of those people came around the corner like that, they were attacking us. No way they killed one of their own."

"The ones we've seen so far have all been male. You think they're killing all the females?" Chris asked.

"Maybe." Jade said. "But why?"

Everyone fell silent.

"Anyone have another explanation?" Chris asked.

"Maybe the virus only infects the males?" Jade suggested.

"So it's a sexist virus?" Frank said. "Damn. Perhaps this Doctor guy has some issues."

"More like he has some daddy issues if he's killing only men," Myles added.

"Guys, knock it off," Chris said. "We don't know how this virus affects people. We have nine bodies in total and have examined none of them yet."

"But it could be true," Frank said.

"Chris is right," Jade said. "We don't know anything yet. What we do know is that we need to secure the lobby before Stevens gets here, so we have a safe area." She stood and pointed to the dead girl on the floor. "I also don't want to end up like her, so can we please get our shit together and move?"

Chris nodded and pointed upwards. "We need to get up to the balcony area in the lobby and seal off any access points. I don't want any of those assholes raining down on us while we work. Worst case scenario, we want them coming only from this hallway. It gives us one entrance to watch and protect, giving us an advantage."

"I'll go pull up a map of the hotel," Myles said, and ran down the hallway back to the lobby.

"Frank, go with him and watch his back," Chris ordered.

He nodded and went after Myles.

Chris and Jade exchanged glances.

"What are you thinking?" Jade asked.

"That we should have prevented this," Chris said.

"Don't blame yourself. We didn't know."

"Yeah, but we should have caught the Doctor before."

"He got away. These things happen. No one's perfect."

"But lives were lost because of my failure."

"*Our* failure," she reminded him. "*We* are a team."

Chris looked at the body in the hallway, then back at the lobby. "All these people."

Jade nodded. "I know."

"Let's head back to the lobby. We need an accurate map of this place so we can close off the upstairs area. Then, we secure the rest of the downstairs, wait for Stevens to show up, and figure out what the hell is going on in this place."

| 4 |

Myles sent the team members a PDF file containing the map of the four-story hotel to their phones.

"Looks like we follow the hallway down to the elevators," Frank said.

"You want to take the elevators?" Myles asked.

Frank shrugged. "Why not?"

"What if the infected people are inside the elevators?" Myles asked. "Or inside the shafts, and they break open the elevator?"

Jade patted Myles on the back, making him jump slightly. "You worry too much. Take the stairs with me."

"I'll go with Frank," Chris said. "Jade, check some rooms along the way. Maybe the Doctor psychopath is hiding out here somewhere. We'll do the same and we'll meet upstairs in the area above the lobby."

"Got it," she said.

"Wait. Here—take these." Myles gave Chris and Frank a key card each. "I made these at the computer. They're basically skeleton keys for the rooms."

Frank's eyes widened. "You mean I can get into any room with this?" he asked, holding up his key card.

Myles nodded.

The two teams separated. Chris and Frank made their way to the elevators while Jade and Myles walked to the end of the hallway towards the staircase.

Frank tapped the elevator button.

"You think we'll find these freaks inside the elevators?" he asked.

Chris shook his head. "I'd be surprised."

The elevator dinged, and the doors opened. Immediately, both men raised their rifles to aim inside the elevator.

It was empty.

They lowered their guns and walked inside the empty elevator. Frank pushed the button for the second floor and the doors closed.

"Ten bucks one of them is waiting outside when we get there," Frank said.

"One of *them,* as in Jade or Myles?" Chris asked.

"No. One of the infected."

The doors dinged.

"You're on," Chris said.

The elevator doors opened. They stepped out into the hallway side by side, guns aimed. Chris looked left while Frank looked to the right. Their eyes darted around as they aimed their weapons down the hallways.

"Clear," Chris said.

"Dammit. Clear," said Frank.

"That'll be ten bucks when we get outta here."

At the end of the hallway to the left was a glass door with the word *Lounge* in black lettering. Chris tapped Frank on the shoulder and pointed.

"Pretty clear messaging on where we need to go."

"Let's check the rooms along the way," Chris said.

There were five rooms—three on the right and two on the left.

They approached the first on their right. Chris took the key card from his leg pouch, then tapped it on the card reader attached to the door. The red light turned green and a *click* came from the lock.

As Chris stepped into the dark room he saw that nothing had been disturbed; the bed was neatly made, the curtains were drawn shut, even the towels were still folded next to the sink. It seemed as though no one had occupied this space recently.

"Nothing here," he said.

Chris headed outside the room, closed the door, and made their way to the door across the hall. Once again, Chris tapped the key card on the card reader and it *clicked.* He grabbed the handle and pushed the door open.

Another dark room. Another untouched bed.

They entered another unoccupied room.

"Empty?" Frank asked.

Chris nodded. He turned towards the door.

"Shit! Frank, look out!"

A figure stood at the entrance, nothing more than a dark silhouette. By its terrifying growls, they realized what it was.

Without hesitation, Frank aimed his weapon and unleashed three shots. The attacker was only able to take a single step forward before collapsing to the ground.

Frank stepped over the dead body and peeked out into the hallway.

"Any more of them?" Chris asked.

"No."

Frank looked down at the body.

"Umm, Chris? You may want to take a look at this."

When Chris made his way to the dead body, he immediately saw why Frank had called him over.

"Female," he said.

Frank nodded. "I guess our earlier hypothesis is out the window, huh?"

"Looks like it."

Chris bent down to examine the body. The woman's blonde hair had blood in it. He raised the woman's head and moved it from side to side before placing it back on the floor. Then he reached into the pockets of her black sweatpants, but found nothing.

"What are you doing?" Frank asked.

"Looking for clues—anything that will give us some idea of what's going on here."

"Find anything?"

"There's blood in her hair." He brushed his hand through it. "It's dry."

"You think it's not hers?" Frank asked. "Maybe she was injured prior?"

Chris looked up at him and shrugged. "Maybe they're killing each other?"

"I have no goddamn idea."

Chris took a deep breath and let out a massive sigh. "What the hell is going on here?"

"Would you like me to repeat my previous statement?"

Chris shook his head. "Jade was right. You *are* an asshole."

"I get that a lot."

Chris dragged the body into the room, then made his way into the hallway. He stared along the hall and back at the door marked *Lounge.*

"Let's open up the rest of these doors and get into the lounge area, "Chris said. "We don't have a lot of time," Chris said.

***

Myles opened the door to the staircase. "Ladies first."

Jade smiled. "You're right. Go ahead."

Myles rolled his eyes. "Ugh. Shut up."

"Come on, Myles. You gotta take a joke sometimes."

"I know, I know... It's just... I've always been picked on. It doesn't help when you guys do it too."

Jade stepped into the stairway. "Look, I know you're young and new to this whole thing."

"That's an understatement," Myles said, following her up the stairs. "You guys have years of experience. Chris just plucked me out of school because I was a genius at computers. He threatened me and then put me in weapons training."

"And you're doing just fine."

"I'm scared shitless."

"To be honest, we all are. No one knows what's going on. That's what this team is all about—*the unknown.* We investigate the strange shit no one else can explain. We're all in this together, okay?" Jade said, trying to reassure Myles.

When she reached the second floor, she turned to face him. "You good?"

He nodded. "Yeah, I'm good."

Slowly, Jade opened the door. Bravely, she stepped out into the hallway and readied her weapon, pointing left and then right, prepared for any threats.

The hallway was empty.

"We're good," she said. "Come on."

Myles crept from behind the door to follow Jade. She stopped at the first door they reached.

"What are you doing?" Myles asked.

"We're checking out the rooms," Jade replied. "Isn't that why you gave us the cards?"

"I didn't think *we* were doing it. I was kind of suggesting that Chris and Frank do it." When Jade didn't respond, he asked, "Can we not, and just say we did?"

"No. Chris tasked us with checking the rooms out, too. Come on." Jade pulled out her key card and tapped it on the card reader. It *clicked.* She pushed the door open.

The interior was dark. She assumed it was an unused room: the bed was neatly made, and not a single thing was out of place.

"Doesn't look occupied," Myles said.

Jade looked around the room one more time. "Doesn't seem like it. Let's check the next room."

As they made their way across the hall, Jade said, "Wouldn't this have been easier if you would have just gotten the list of where all the guests were staying, so we only had to check those rooms?"

"And what makes you think some staff member isn't in another unoccupied room? Or that the guest list is accurate? Someone may have changed rooms. Maybe someone or *something* broke into another room? Maybe—"

"Okay, I get it," Jade said, interrupting him. She put the key card on the digital pad, unlocked the door, and pushed it open.

Another dark room.

The bed was made. Nothing was out of place, just as in the previous room. But then Jade noticed something in the corner.

A travel bag.

"Myles, hold up," she said.

"What is it?" he asked.

Jade shushed him and raised her gun. She crept around the room, aiming her weapon in all directions. Then she made her way to the foot of the bed. With swift precision, her gun instantly shifted to point at the side of the bed hidden from her view.

There was no one was there.

Satisfied, she made her way to the windows and opened the blinds. Dust particles were illuminated by the police floodlights outside beaming through the windows.

"What?" Myles asked.

"This was someone's room," Jade said.

"Okay? And? What makes you think they're still here?"

"I don't know. I just noticed the bag."

"Do you think they're still here?"

"Myles, *I don't know.* I'm examining this room for the first time."

A noise came from the bathroom. It sounded as if something had fallen to the floor.

They both turned and aimed their weapons at the bathroom door.

"What was that?" Myles asked.

"Myles, I swear. One more question and I'm going to shoot you myself."

Whispers came from the bathroom.

Jade glanced at Myles and put her index finger to her lips. She moved to the bathroom door, her gun trained on it. She reached for the doorknob and twisted it, then swung the door open quickly and aimed the gun inside.

Screams came from the bathtub.

Quickly, Jade pulled the curtain aside.

"Oh, shit," she said.

"What?" Myles asked from outside the bathroom.

Jade stared into the bathtub. She couldn't believe her eyes.

"We have survivors."

| 5 |

Jade lowered her weapon. "Are you okay?"

The woman in the bathtub had a child wrapped in her arms. She wore black sweatpants with a white sweatshirt. She tucked her head into the little girl's shoulders and squeezed tighter. The woman's brown hair dripped down in front of her face and onto the little girl's head, as if shielding her.

"Ma'am, I'm not here to hurt you," Jade said. "I'm here to help. We're working with the local authorities. Are you guys okay?" She got down on one knee and said softly, "Ma'am, we're here to help you."

Slowly, the woman lifted her head up and brushed her hair out of her face.

Jade offered a small smile. "My name is Jade Burleigh. That scaredy cat over there is Myles Johnson."

"Hey!" Myles said.

Jade turned to look at him. "What? Prove me wrong." She faced the woman in the bathtub. "What are your names?"

The woman's blue eyes darted between Jade and Myles. She kept the child wrapped tight in her arms.

"Why are you wearing those suits?" the woman asked.

"We believe a pathogen has been released inside this hotel," Jade said. "These suits are for our protection. We're here trying to figure out what's going on."

"A pathogen?" the woman asked.

"A virus. A terrorist released a virus inside this hotel."

"Are we going to die?"

"No, ma'am. We're here to get you to safety," Jade reassured her.

In all honesty, she didn't believe that, but she knew it would calm the woman down and get her to do exactly what Jade needed.

Jade extended her hand. The woman trembled slightly, but not nearly as much as before. Slowly, her arms uncoiled from around the child and she reached for Jade's hand. With a firm grip, Jade pulled the woman to a standing position. The child stood up as well, this time clutching the woman's leg.

"What are your names?" Jade asked again.

"My name is Ellen. This is my daughter, Caroline."

"It's nice to meet both of you," Jade said. Caroline let go as Jade helped the woman step out of the bathtub, then extended her arms for her mom to pick her up.

"I like your pajamas," Jade said to Caroline, who was wearing pink pajamas covered in cartoon princesses. Jade gave her a polite smile and then asked Ellen, "How old is Caroline?"

Ellen picked up her daughter and lifted her out of the tub, placing her on the floor. "She's seven."

"You're such a brave young woman," Jade said to Caroline. "Are you taking care of your mom here?"

Again, Caroline hid behind her mother's leg.

"She's usually more outgoing, but you can understand her reason for hiding right now," Ellen said.

"I completely understand," Jade said. "Myles and I are here to protect you guys."

Three gunshots echoed in the hallway. Caroline let out a brief scream behind her mom's legs.

"Myles, go check on that," Jade said.

Myles nodded and left the bathroom.

Jade kneeled down and said to Caroline, "Don't be afraid. There are two other men with us that have guns. What you heard was them protecting us." She looked up at Ellen. "I don't want to alarm you guys, but there is something dangerous happening in this hotel."

"You mean those people randomly attacking and killing other people?" Ellen asked.

Myles returned. "Nothing in the hallway. Sounded like it came from where Chris and Frank are."

"We should probably get moving then," Jade said.

"Wait," Ellen said. "We're going out there?"

"Yes. We have to meet up with the rest of our team."

Myles moved to the doorway, glancing in both directions as Jade ushered Ellen and Caroline out of the room. The pair clasped hands tightly as they made their way along the corridor. At the corner, Myles moved ahead to peek around it.

"Clear," he said.

Jade took the lead again, keeping Ellen and her daughter close.

"Back in the room, you said people were randomly attacking and killing people," Jade said. "What did you mean by that?"

"People just started attacking one another," Ellen replied.

"When did this happen?"

"A few hours ago? I'm not really sure."

"Daddy got mean, and we had to run," Caroline said.

"Shh," Ellen said. "We'll find Daddy later."

Jade whispered to Ellen, "Was he infected?"

Ellen shrugged. "I don't know what happened. One minute we were walking to the lobby, talking. The next moment, he started screaming. He pushed Caroline to the ground and slammed me into the wall."

"I'm sorry," Jade said.

"I tried pleading with him. I had no idea what had just happened. He just snapped. He was fine a second before he acted like that."

"So what happened to him after that?"

"I don't know. He went down after I kicked him in the groin. I grabbed my daughter. We ran back to our room and locked the door."

Jade nodded. "Well, I'm glad you guys could get away and stay safe."

They made their way to the glass door with *Lounge* written on it. Jade readied herself as she opened the door. She was immediately met with two gun barrels pointing directly at her face. She aimed her own weapon in front of her.

***

"Don't aim that shit at me," Frank said.

"I only did because you did," Jade responded.

They all lowered their weapons.

Chris and Frank each took a second glance as Ellen and Caroline entered the room, their faces filled with intrigue and curiosity.

Chris spoke first. "Who are they?"

"This is Ellen and her daughter, Caroline," Jade said. "Myles and I found them in one of the rooms back by the stairs."

"And they're not infected?" Frank asked.

"No, Frank," she said." They're fine,"

"If they're not infected, then we're good here, right?" he said. "Can we take these hazmat suits off? I'm sweating my balls off in this thing."

"No," Chris replied. "They stay on. We know nothing yet."

"Are we infected?" Ellen asked.

"Ma'am, we don't know what's going on here yet," Chris said. "We only stepped inside the hotel a few moments ago. Technically, we're the first responders."

"We don't know if you've been exposed," Jade added. "We have someone coming soon with some equipment to test the air here. Soon we'll find out if the virus is still present.

Ellen nodded hesitantly. Her hands were balled into fists and shook. She looked down at her daughter, whose arms were still wrapped around her mom's legs. Ellen ran her fingers through her daughter's hair.

"Mommy, when are we going to leave?" Caroline asked.

Ellen forced a smile. "Soon, honey. As soon as these nice people help us out."

Chris couldn't help but feel sorry for them. This family had been ripped apart by this virus.

"Alright guys," he said. "We need to close this area down. It looks like the only way in or out is through that door. We need to seal it off somehow."

"We can shove some furniture against the door as a barrier," Myles suggested.

"We should probably do something to blockade the hallway too," Jade said.

"Good. Frank, go with Jade and help her set up a barricade down the hallway," Chris said. "I'll stay here with Myles and take care of this side, and Ellen and her daughter can keep us company."

"Sounds good," Jade said. "Come on, Frank. Let's go."

"I gotta team up with you?" he asked.

"I mean, you don't have to. You take your pick. An old man and a computer nerd with a gun, or me."

"Can I go alone?"

"Chris," Jade said. "Frank says he wants to go alone."

"No lone wolfing it, Frank. You hear me?" Chris said.

"Guess you're stuck with me," Jade said.

"Considering my options, you're the best choice," Frank replied.

"Aww, you're so sweet."

"You better shut the hell up and keep walking out that door. That's the only *sweet* thing you'll hear from me."

Jade opened the glass door and her and Frank stepped into the hallway.

| 6 |

Frank stormed inside the first room with his rifle aimed into the darkness.

Jade stepped inside and turned on the lights. "This usually helps."

Frank faced Jade and rolled his eyes at her. Seeing no one was in the room, he lowered his weapon. He pulled the sheets off the bed and threw them into the corner of the room.

Jade opened the dresser drawers, tossing any contents onto the floor.

"Come help me with this," she said.

"Too weak to move furniture by yourself?" Frank asked.

"No, smartass. More like, it's too big for one person to move."

"You weakling. You get the mattress, I'll take the dresser. Get out of my way," he said, shoving her to one side.

Frank was determined to move the massive dresser by himself, tugging and pushing it with all his might. However, no matter how hard he tried, he could only manage a few inches at a time before having to pause. Jade watched on silently with her arms crossed and an amused smirk on her face, conveying a silent mockery of his labors. Cursing under his breath, Frank gritted his teeth and gathered all his available strength in one last effort to move it solo.

"Looks like you need some help, Frank," Jade said.

"Shut up and grab the other side," Frank said.

The pair worked together to move the dresser outside the room and place it against the glass door. They walked back inside the hotel room and grabbed the mattress.

"So I guess our idea about the virus only affecting men was accurate, since Ellen and her daughter Caroline are uninfected," Jade said.

They began twisting the mattress to fit through the door frame.

"Nope. I killed a woman earlier, when I was with Chris."

Jade dropped her side of the mattress.

"What the hell?" Frank said.

"Seriously?" Jade asked. "There was a woman infected?"

"Yes. Now, would you pick up your side?"

They continued moving the mattress, placing it against the door, then returned to the room.

"Should we take these too?" Frank asked, gesturing at the table and chairs in the corner of the room.

"Take everything. I'd like it if the whole hallway was full of this stuff."

Frank picked up the table while Jade took the two chairs.

"So how come Ellen and Caroline weren't infected?" Frank asked. "Did they say anything to you?"

"I don't know. Ellen's husband must have been, though. She said he tried to attack them. They got away and ran to their room."

"Were they all together when the infection happened?"

"She said they were walking down the hallway and it just suddenly happened."

They placed the furniture against the mattress.

"Weird," Frank said.

***

"Myles, help me lift this," Chris said.

They had started moving the tables and chairs in front of the door, blocking it. Chris was currently trying to move a love seat.

"You think this will hold those infected people back?" Myles asked.

Together, they carried the love seat to the door and dropped it.

"Based on all the stuff we have here," Chris said, gesturing at the two chairs, a table, and a love seat, "I think we're good. Plus, Jade and Frank are on the other side doing the same thing."

Chris tapped the side of his hood. They all wore earpieces to communicate with each other. "You guys okay over there?"

Jade replied, "Yeah. Frank and I have emptied almost three rooms. I'd say we're pretty good here."

"No run-ins with anyone?" Chris asked.

"Nope. Quiet on this side."

"Good. Let me know if anything changes."

"Understood," Jade said.

"Sir," Ellen said.

"You can call me Chris."

She gave a faint smile. "Chris, can you tell me what's going on here?"

Chris hesitated, unsure what to tell her. Then again, she had already been living through the events within the hotel.

"Ellen, you've been here longer than we have. You had an experience with your husband becoming infected. What can you tell me about what you've seen here?"

She shrugged. "Pretty sure I told you guys everything already."

"Did you see or hear anything when you were in your room?"

***

Ellen remembered being curled up behind the bed with her daughter crying next to her. She had constantly told her daughter to remain quiet. They had tried to keep their breathing to a minimum to be as silent as possible. Ellen had been terrified as she held Caroline in her arms. Her daughter had been rigid and pale.

Ellen didn't remember how long she had stayed tucked behind the bed, but she remembered switching hiding spots when something banged against the wall. They fell to the ground in fear.

Then came the screams. The awful, blood-curdling screams. Someone was dying. In a moment of panic, Ellen had scooped up her daughter and raced to the nearest safe haven: the bathroom. Together, they slid into the tub and Ellen hoped the curtains would keep them hidden.

***

Finally, Ellen said, "The screams. I remember screaming."

"Where were the screams coming from?" Chris asked.

"I don't know. I think in the room next to us. It sounded like someone was being murdered."

Chris sighed. "I'm sorry you and your daughter have to go through this terrible ordeal." He glanced at Caroline, who was sitting by the railing, dangling her feet over the ledge. "She seems to be doing okay despite everything going on."

Ellen looked at her daughter. "Yeah. She's tough for her age. A few years ago, she fell out of her crib and broke her arm. Snapped the bone. Her arm was dangling, like she had another elbow in her forearm. It scared the crap out of me. She cried at first, either because of the pain—or fear. I'm not really sure. She was only two. But once I got her into the car and started driving to the hospital, she was fine. She sat in her seat staring out the window and asking if she was going to be okay."

"That must have been difficult for you. Where was your husband?"

"At work. He worked about an hour away. Pretty sure it took him half that time to get to us that day. He must have sped like crazy to get to the hospital." Ellen smiled. "He was so worried about her." Her smile faded.

Chris put his hand on her shoulder. "We still don't exactly know what we're dealing with yet, but we should have a better idea soon. We'll find your husband. Maybe there's a way to save him."

She nodded. "Thanks. I hope so."

As Chris went back to helping Myles, he looked at Caroline sitting by the railing, kicking her dangling legs back and forth. Ellen sat down to join her.

Chris became heartbroken for the separated family. He truly wished there was something he could do for them. He hoped they'd find an answer to what was happening soon.

* * *

"I feel like I'm arguing with my brother," Jade said.

Frank dropped the chair he had been holding, and spun to face Jade. "You and your brother argued while roaming the infected hallways of hotels, carrying furniture, wearing hazmat suits, armed with multiple weapons, and you went around shooting people who made funny faces at you?"

Jade tried to hold it back, but a smile appeared on her face. "I hate you."

Frank picked up the chair and continued on. "I know."

Faint screams stopped them both in their tracks.

"You hear that?" Frank asked.

"Yeah," Jade said.

There were more screams—louder this time.

"They're getting closer," Jade said.

She aimed her gun towards the end of the hallway. Suddenly, three figures came sprinting frantically along the hallway, fearful shouts echoing from the walls.

Jade almost fired, but held back. These people were fleeing from something. They weren't infected. They were more survivors.

A flash darted across the hallway, towards the survivors.

"That was an infected," Jade said. "They're in trouble. We have to go help."

Frank nodded and then started running down the hallways after them.

"What was that?" Chris said over the Jade's earpiece.

Jade tapped her earpiece and replied, "We found more survivors. They're being pursued by infected. We're heading after them now."

Jade and Frank stopped in response to a ferocious growl. A man stood at the end of the hallway dressed in only a bathing suit, blocking their progress. The snarl and crazed eyes were distinct signs that he was infected. He leaned forward, ready to attack.

Frank leaned forward, too, and matched the sound of the snarl, imitating it. Before the infected could take a single step towards them, Frank hurled a chair at him. Upon impact, it smashed into three pieces, and the man was left dazed. He fell to the ground, but got back to his feet immediately.

"I guess pain doesn't slow them down all that much," Jade said.

"No, but this will." Frank aimed and fired a bullet into the head of the infected. He went down instantly and stopped moving.

"Another one bites the dust," Frank said.

"Come on, let's keep moving!" Jade said.

***

"What's happening over there?" Chris asked. "I heard gunshots."

Jade's voice came over the earpiece. "We ran into an infected. Took care of it. We're on our way to the other survivors now."

The screams sounded louder to Chris now.

"I see people down there," Caroline said.

Chris and Myles ran to the railing.

Three people were running desperately towards the front door of the lobby. One of them stumbled and slid across the tiled floor. As he attempted to climb to his feet again, an infected pounced on him, slamming him back to the ground.

"Nick! No!" the woman by the front door screamed.

She tried to reach out to the fallen man, but the man standing beside her held her back.

The infected pounded on the helpless man on the ground. Despite his frantic attempts to escape, the infected grabbed his head and repeatedly smashed it onto the floor.

With a single well-aimed head shot, Chris ended the infected's rampage. It flinched and crumpled to the floor.

The two people at the front door spotted Chris above. They spun around and pulled on the locked door.

"It's locked," Chris yelled to them.

"We need to get out! There are more coming!" the man yelled back.

The woman beside him screamed, and the man next to her pointed back to the hallway.

Chris looked to where the man pointed and assumed he could see other infected coming down the hallway towards them.

"Myles, lay down cover fire for them," Chris said. "You see those things coming—shoot them!"

Myles nodded.

Quickly, Chris scanned the lounge area for a way to make his descent. With no time on his side, tossing cushions over the edge to provide a soft landing was out of the question. Then his gaze settled on an unlikely solution—a retractable stanchion. Chris hurried over and grabbed it before making his way to the railing.

Myles fired four shots next to Chris, startling him for a split second. Chris looked at the lobby and saw one of the infected stumble to the floor.

Chris shoved the round base of the stanchion between the railing and then unspooled the retractable rope from the post, which he wound around his hands, giving him a strong grip.

Myles fired another few shots, taking down two more infected.

Chris took a deep breath. He was getting too old for these types of maneuvers. His heart raced as he prepared to jump. He stopped working himself up and then jumped over the railing. The retractable rope begun spooling from the post as Chris descended to the lobby floor.

The rope locked into place. It pulled the base up to the railing where it became stuck between the posts.

Chris ended up swinging beneath the overhang and happen to kick one of the infected in its head. His grip loosened, and then suddenly he was landing on the floor—with a painful *thud,* that knocked the wind out of him. His gun had slipped off his shoulder and slid a few feet away. He groaned in pain.

The infected, a young male, possibly in his twenties, got back to his feet before Chris did. He let out a harrowing scream as he pounced towards Chris, who grabbed his sidearm and fired four shots in quick succession. The body landed lifelessly on top of him.

He brushed the body off and climbed to his feet. Before he had time to register what had just happened, three more infected burst into the lobby with murderous intent written across their faces.

Chris aimed his gun at the infected sprinting towards him, but before he could fire, two of them dropped to the ground like rag dolls. Chris shifted his aim to the one that remained, and fired two shots, hitting him in the chest and head. The infected stumbled backwards and fell.

Jade and Frank emerged from the hallway and scanned the lobby.

"Everyone okay?" Jade asked.

"Yeah," Chris replied.

The woman by the front door finally freed herself from the man holding her back. She ran over to the body on the floor, her baggy sweatshirt flapping with every step she took. She slid to a stop, kneeling down a few feet from him. The man lay in a pool of his own blood. She covered her face with her hands and wept, her brown hair falling in front of her face, providing a layer to hide behind.

Chris crouched beside the body and reached for the man's carotid artery to confirm the man was dead.

The second man, who wore jeans and a black T-shirt, made his way to the woman.

"Are you two okay?" Chris asked.

The man nodded. "Thank you for saving our lives."

The woman continued crying.

"Is she going to be okay?" Chris asked.

The man put his arm around her. "We were all friends. Nick and Emily were friends for like twenty years."

"I'm sorry for your loss, Emily," Chris said, trying to get her attention.

She removed her hands from her face and finally spoke. "What the hell is going on here? Why are these people killing everyone? And why are you wearing that?" Tears ran down her face, smearing her makeup.

Chris explained that a virus had been released inside the hotel. He stood up and offered his hand to Emily, who was still sitting on the floor. She took his hand and helped her to her feet.

"I'm Chris Hoffman," he said. He pointed to Jade and Frank introducing them. He looked around but couldn't see Myles.

"I'm up here," Myles said, waving from the balcony. "Don't worry, though. I'm okay. Thanks for asking."

Ellen and her daughter, Caroline, peeked over the railing as well, looking down at the carnage below. She pulled her daughter back away from the railing, disappearing from sight.

"I'm James," the man by the front door said.

"Nice to meet you guys," Chris said.

Frank and Jade made their way past the bodies to approach Chris.

"So what's next?" Frank asked.

Everyone became startled as three loud knocks came from the front lobby door, sending James bolting away.

"Uh, hello? It's Stevens," a muffled voice said from the other side of the door. He knocked three more times.

Chris pulled a set of keys from the pouch on his leg and inserted the correct one into the lock, then opened the door.

James ran for the door.

"Hey!" Jade yelled.

Frank stuck out his foot and tripped him. James went tumbling and slid into one of the corpses of the infected. Staring in horror at what he had just touched, he scrambled backwards until he was planted next to Frank's legs.

Frank dangled his handgun in his left hand. "Don't make me use this on you. I'd kind of like to use the bullets on those infected bastards."

"Frank," Chris said, "put the gun away." He looked down at James. "No one leaves. Not yet, anyway. We are in quarantine until we know exactly what's going on."

Chris opened the door, and a man in a hazmat suit entered. He wore glasses and under the plastic shield a mustache was visible. He held a duffel bag in his left hand.

"Hey, Chris," he said, dropping the bag at his feet. He looked around at the blood and corpses. "Looks like you guys have been busy."

Chris closed the door and locked it, then returned the keys to the pouch on his leg.

Stevens noticed James and Emily. He pointed to them. "Who are they?"

"Survivors," Jade said.

"Survivors?" Stevens replied.

Chris nodded. "Yes, there are uninfected in here."

Stevens looked at the two people without hazmat suits.

"Chris, I need to talk to you," Stevens said. "Privately."

The pair walked to one end of the lobby.

"What's going on, Stevens?" Chris asked.

Stevens looked back at the rest of the group before replying. "These people without the hazmat suits are infected. They have to be."

"What do you mean?" Chris asked. "They seem fine."

"Maybe. What if they're not? How is it that they're not infected, but many others are?"

Chris shrugged. "You tell me. That's why you're here."

"Based on my findings so far, I just can't see how they could have avoided being infected."

"What findings?"

"I examined one of the bodies outside, and found traces of a pathogen in their mouth, throat and up their nose."

"What does that mean?" Chris asked.

"It means they ingested it. Breathed it in. Inhaled it. Possibly still breathing it in. It's in the air."

Chris glanced around the lobby to see if he could see the virus in the air.

"I don't know if it's still live in the air now," Stevens said. "That's what I'm here to find out. But, if it *was* in the air earlier, there's no doubt in my mind that these people have it in their system. One way or another, they're probably infected."

| 7 |

Myles was sitting on the ground alone, exhausted. Each time he took on a mission, restlessness the night before would keep him up at all hours of the night. Now, his tiredness had finally caught up with him.

He put his hands behind his head and laid down. He told himself he should stand up, but he ignored the idea. It felt too good to relax. His eyelids were heavy, and the thought of a nap felt comforting. He closed his eyes.

Myles heard footsteps walking towards him. He could sense someone staring at him. All he wanted to do was take a quick nap. Was that too much to ask?

He opened his eyes and saw Caroline standing next to him. "What?" he asked.

"What's your favorite color?" she asked.

He was taken aback, confused by her random question.

He shook his head. "What's my favorite...what?" he repeated.

"What's your favorite color?" she asked again. "Mine is pink. My daddy painted my room pink when I was a baby. My mom said she wants to change it. But I like it."

Myles smiled and sat up. He couldn't believe that despite everything that was going on, this little girl was talking to him about favorite colors.

The true innocence of a child, he thought.

"If I had to pick, I'd choose green as my favorite color," Myles told her.

Caroline's eyes widened. "I like green too! That's my second favorite color. What's your second favorite color?"

"Honey, why don't you leave the poor man alone, okay?" Ellen said.

"But Mommy..." Caroline whined.

"Come over here and help me with something," Ellen requested.

Caroline sighed, got up, and joined her mom.

Myles rose to his feet, taking a moment to stretch out the stiffness in his muscles. In search of some motivation and energy, he walked over to the railing and observed everyone below.

"You guys need anything, or can I go take a nap?" he said.

Chris and Stevens were alone in a corner of the lobby. Frank and Jade stood together, with James still at Frank's feet.

"If I see you with your eyes closed, consider yourself issued an official invitation to join the ranks of those poor infected assholes," Frank said.

"Well, now I know who *not* to go to for bedtime stories," Myles said.

Chris and Stevens made their way back to the group.

***

"Guys, listen up. Here's what's going on," Chris said. "I think we can all agree the pathogen had to have been released somewhere in this hotel. But we don't know where to look or what we're looking for. The virus is airborne. He examined one of the bodies outside—"

Stevens butted in. "The body had traces of something unknown in the nose and mouth, leading me to believe the virus was released in the air."

"The Doctor must have placed the device of origin somewhere where it would easily travel throughout the building," Chris said. "We need to find out where it is."

"Do we know what we're looking for?" Jade asked.

"No," Stevens said. "It could be as small as a test tube or something larger like a box or a suitcase."

"Doc, we're in a hotel. There are a lot of things like that," Frank said.

"I know. But we're looking for something placed somewhere where it would easily spread throughout the entire building," Stevens said.

"What about the lobby? Kind of a central place, right?" Frank said.

"Yeah, but where in here would he be able to release it so it would spread throughout the hotel in a matter of minutes... or seconds?" Stevens said.

"Geez, doc. A simple *no* would have worked better," Frank said.

Jade glanced up at Myles. He was fixated on the ceiling.

"Myles, what are you looking at?" Jade asked.

The rest of the team looked at Myles above them, and followed his gaze to the ceiling.

He dropped his attention to the group in the first-floor lobby. "Air vents," he said.

"What?" Frank asked.

Myles pulled out his phone and opened up the blueprints for the building that he had downloaded earlier.

"It would be the quickest way to disperse the virus throughout the entire building in a short amount of time," Stevens said.

"But there are air vents all over the hotel. Where would we know where the device is?" Chris asked.

"In the basement," Myles said.

Everyone focused on Myles again.

He continued, "According to the blueprints, there's a door down the hall, towards the elevators. It may say *Staff* or something like that on it. That'll lead to the basement, where all the electrical and ventilation systems are. That's where the generator is, and it's most likely where whatever device you're looking for will be."

"Looks like we're heading to the basement," Chris said.

"Me?" Myles asked.

"No. You're our eyes and ears up above. You can see everything from up there. And I think you're pretty secure there too." Chris pointed to Jade. "You're coming with me and Stevens."

Jade nodded.

"Frank, I need you to watch the lobby. Protect those two over there." He gestured at Emily and James. "And if any more infected people come in here, you know what to do."

"No!" Stevens objected.

"What do you mean, no?" Chris asked.

"Yeah," Frank said. "You better explain why I can't kill those things that are trying to kill me."

"We don't know if this is a permanent infection," Stevens said. "Maybe we can cure them. And according to my most recent studies, we can't cure *death.*"

"So you're telling me that if one of those murdering lunatics comes towards me, I'm supposed to talk to it?" Frank said. "Tell it '*Please, no running in the hallways*? You're out of your damn mind if you think I'm not going to shoot anything that charges at me with a monstrous snarl on its face."

"He's got a point, Doc," Chris said.

Stevens sighed. "Okay, look—if it's life or death, I understand. But otherwise, please try to avoid killing them."

"I'll be as friendly as I can be with them," Frank said.

Jade chuckled.

He turned to face her. "Is that funny to you?"

"Yeah. You being *friendly* is something I'd really like to see."

"Aww, well, it's too bad you're going on that scavenger hunt to the basement. Otherwise, you may have had your chance."

"Damn. I was looking forward to it."

Chris gave a disinterested sigh. "I work with children." He walked towards the hallway and gestured to his team. "Let's go."

| 8 |

"Ready?" Chris asked.

Jade had her weapon in hand, while Stevens gripped his bag. A nod from each of them was all that was needed to show Chris they were prepared.

Chris opened the basement door, leading into blackness. He searched the wall next to him but found no light switch, so he stepped into the dark void and felt around with his foot before descending the staircase.

"Stevens," Chris said, "move up with me." He reached into his leg pouch and pulled out a small flashlight, which he handed to Stevens. "Take this and give me some light."

"This little thing? Doesn't seem—" He stopped as he turned it on. "Oh wow. That's bright."

Stevens remained directly behind Chris as they descended the staircase. Jade followed behind them. They took each step slowly, attempting to make as little noise as possible.

At the bottom of the staircase, the hallway angled to the right. A light came from the far end. Chris put his back against the wall and peeked along the corridor.

Infected were wandering around the hallway—at least ten of them.

Chris spun back around.

"We have a problem," he said.

"What?" Jade asked.

"It looks like there's about ten infected down the hallway," Chris said.

"So? We have guns."

"No killing," Stevens said.

"Are we really sticking to that?" she asked.

"Yes," Stevens said. "What if this virus isn't permanent? Maybe it's temporary. Maybe we can cure them."

"And what if we can't?" she said.

"That's a bridge we'll cross when we have more information," Stevens replied.

Jade shook her head. "Whatever. I don't agree with it. So, then if you don't want us killing them, how do you propose we get around them?"

Stevens leaned past Chris to look along the hallway.

"I don't know," he whispered.

* * *

"Do you want to play I-spy?" Caroline asked.

"Honey, I asked you to leave the nice man alone," Ellen said.

Myles waved her off. "No, it's okay." He looked at Caroline. "Sure, I'll play."

"Nerd!" Frank yelled from below.

Myles ignored him. "Go ahead."

"You go first," Caroline said.

Myles smiled. "Okay." He looked around. "I spy something... black."

"Hmm. Is it your suit?"

Myles shook his head.

"How about your gun?"

He shook his head again.

"Your soul!" Frank yelled.

"I thought you weren't playing?" he yelled back.

"Your soul?" Caroline asked Myles.

Frank broke out into laughter.

"Don't listen to him," he told Caroline. "He's an idiot. And *no*, it's not my *soul*."

"And I called you a nerd. I didn't say I wasn't playing," Frank said.

"Umm..." Caroline said, looking around. She looked down at her shoes. "My shoes?"

Myles nodded. "Yup."

Caroline smiled. "My turn!" She made her way to the railing and said, "I spy something red."

"Well, it's pretty obvious you're looking over the railing at something, so that eliminates all of this," Myles said, waving an arm. He stood up and walked to the railing, then knew what she must have been looking at. He hoped he was wrong.

He hesitated before saying, "Is... is it the blood on the floor?"

"No, silly." She shook her head and pointed. "The magazine on the table down there."

Myles' heart sunk to his stomach briefly.

"Myles, did you seriously ask that poor girl if what she spied was all the blood on the floor? You're sick," Frank said.

"What did you think she was looking at?" Myles replied.

"I wasn't playing, so I don't have to answer. Like I said—nerd."

"Are you always this immature?" Emily said as she walked past Frank.

"The simple answer is yes," Frank said.

"What's the more complicated answer?" she asked him.

He thought for a second. "Yes, *I am.*"

Frank caught her smirk as she walked away. "I saw that. You laughed."

Emily shook her head and walked to James and sat alongside him on the floor by the reception desk. Frank noticed the two of them begin to whisper to each other. He wondered what they were discussing.

"Frank!"

He shook his head, jolting himself out of his train of thought.

"What the hell are you doing?" Myles asked. "Looks like you're the one falling asleep standing up."

"What do you want, nerd?"

"Do you think they're okay? Chris, Jade, and Stevens?"

Frank shrugged his shoulders. "I'd guess so. I haven't heard any communication from them and we haven't heard a gun go off."

That made Myles feel a little better. He was a little worried about splitting everyone up, especially since he was up above in the lounge.

He turned to find Caroline standing in front of him.

"Wanna play again?" she asked.

He smiled. This girl knew how to distract him.

"Sure."

***

Chris stared at his phone, looking at the PDF of the building Myles had sent him earlier.

"If we're here," he said, pointing to the tiny screen, "then there should be a door around this corner leading to a room... or a closet." He turned the corner carefully, trying to avoid attracting attention. He saw the door on the right, but it was too far to sneak down the hallway without being detected.

He turned towards Stevens and Jade. "Okay, I found the room, but there's no way to get there without being seen."

"Can we get them to go further down the hall somehow?" Stevens asked.

"How?" Chris asked.

"I'll do it," Jade asked.

Simultaneously, Chris and Stevens asked, "Do what?"

"We all can't sneak down together, right?" Jade said. "So, I'll go. Give me the bag and tell me what I have to do."

"It's not that easy," Stevens said.

"Sure it is," Jade replied. She stuck out her hand. "Bag, please."

Stevens looked at Chris. "You can't expect her to do this."

"If there's anyone who I trust to get this done, and done right, it's Jade. Give her the bag."

Stevens handed Jade the bag. She swung it over her shoulder.

"Here goes nothing," she whispered to herself, and then left her hiding spot. She crept along the hallway, weapon ready, keeping close to the wall.

Chris and Stevens watched from their position of safety. They held their breath in anticipation, hoping Jade would make it safely, alerting none of the infected.

***

Jade approached the door, finally arriving at her destination. With her heart racing and nerves running high, she hurried into the room. As soon as she shut the door behind her, she let out a sigh of relief and leaned against the door.

A growl startled her.

Her eyes widened. She scanned the dim room, then pulled out her flashlight, illuminating every inch of it.

To her right, one of the infected snarled. Without warning, it rushed at her.

| 9 |

A sense of relief washed over Chris as he watched Jade slip down the hallway unseen and close the door behind her.

Chris glanced at the map on his phone.

"Okay, now that she's in there, she'll have to climb up into the ceiling and come down to the other side of the wall. The ventilation system is on the other side of that room," he said.

"I hope you're right about her," Stevens said.

"I am."

A loud scream came from the room Jade had entered.

Chris turned the corner and noticed the infected had heard it, too. The infected were now heading towards the door in a frenzy, pushing each other aside.

"Shit," Chris said. He tapped his ear. "Jade, you okay? You're about to have company."

He aimed his rifle around the corner.

"No killing them," Stevens repeated.

Chris's lip curled. "If one of them enters that room, I'm opening fire."

***

The infected leaped towards Jade. A split second later, she was thrown violently to the floor. Knowing every second mattered, she threw an elbow fiercely into its face in order to try and create some space between them. The infected's head wrenched to one side in response to the blow, then delivered a terrifying scream in Jade's face, seemingly unfazed by the attack.

The infected was a man wearing a rumpled grey suit. His white buttoned-up shirt had a few holes in it. The man's tattered jacket dangled over Jade as he tried to slam his fists at her face.

Jade rolled out of the way just as his fists came crashing down. Regaining her footing, she began her attack with a powerful kick to the infected's head that sent him sprawling onto the floor. He looked up at her, yelling furiously like some feral animal.

"Jade, you okay?" a familiar voice echoed in her earpiece. "You're about to have some company."

I guess the noise alerted the other infected outside, she thought. *No need to be quiet anymore.*

She pulled out her handgun, aimed it at the monster in front of her, and fired. A single gunshot to his head silenced the infected man, and he collapsed.

"How long?" she said.

"Maybe five or six seconds."

She heard Stevens, trying to talk over Chris, asking if she had just shot the infected.

Jade scanned the room and spotted a chair tucked behind a desk. She grabbed it and rushed back to the door, then wedged the chair beneath the handle, hoping to create a barricade.

As she released her grip on the chair, the handle wiggled. Suddenly, a monstrous force was hammering against the door with such ferocity that it seemed as if they'd break through any second, rendering the chair completely useless.

"Where am I going?" she asked.

"There should be a drop ceiling. Climb up and make your way over to the room next to you. That should be where the ventilation system is," Chris said.

Jade gazed up and saw what he meant. As the adrenaline pulsing through her veins, she raced to the desk and scaled it before propelling herself upwards with a mighty leap, knocking a ceiling tile away. With each passing second, the threatening growls from behind the door became more intense. No matter how brave Jade pretended to act around everyone else, this was true terror like no other. She didn't want to be ripped apart by those seething monsters.

She swung the bag off her shoulder and tossed it up into the ceiling.

The door shook violently and slipped off its top hinge. The infected were starting to get through. She had to hurry.

She reached up, but the ceiling remained just beyond her reach. She leaped in an attempt to grab hold of it, but dropped back onto the desk.

Loud cracking noises came from the door. The chair beneath the handle started to snap. Jade could now see a gap in the doorway.

Her survival was at stake and those things were about to break down that door. She had only seconds left.

With a final leap, Jade grabbed onto the opening in the ceiling she had made, and pulled herself up.

"I'm in," she said into her earpiece.

A moment later, the door broke down and all Jade could hear was the heavy stomping of the swarming infected entering the room below her. Jade lay flat on her back, hoping nothing else would go wrong. She took out her flashlight, its beam slicing through the darkness to illuminate countless wires and pipes above her. Jade grabbed the bag and began to crawl towards the next room.

***

Chris spun back around the corner. He rested his head against the wall and closed his eyes for a few seconds, composing himself before he spoke to Stevens.

"This is my mission. These are my people," he said. "I don't know why I listened to you about not shooting those things. They almost killed one of my team members."

"Right—*almost.* But they—" Stevens began.

"No!" Chris interrupted him in an intense whisper. "I don't want to hear about this *almost* shit. You're lucky Jade's alive right now. I don't want to hear another order from you. You're not in charge. I am. This is *my* team and its members are *my* responsibility—not yours. You want to go find some infected and try to save them? Go for it. I'm not risking the lives of my team again over it. Understand?"

Stevens was taken aback; after all their years of friendship, he couldn't believe Chris was speaking to him in such an uncharacteristically harsh tone.

"I got it. I'm sorry," he said.

"I don't want to hear your apologies. Let's get out of here first, and then you can apologize all you want."

Stevens nodded.

***

As Jade carefully maneuvered her way through the ceiling, Chris's voice transmitted in her earpiece. "Jade, you read me?"

"Yeah, I'm here," she replied.

"Where are you now?"

"Still in the ceiling. I'm crawling over to the room now. But it's dark up here. I don't know where I'm supposed to drop to. Also, I'm not trying to disturb those infected I left behind."

"Have you gone far? Try lifting one of the ceiling tiles up to see where you are."

"Hold on," she said.

Jade crawled over one more tile and placed the bag next to her. She hung the flashlight above her on a dangling wire. She lifted the ceiling tile slightly and peeked below.

A giant machine was pressed up against a wall. She had found the right room. She moved the tile to one side and examined the room.

"I'm here," Jade said. "There's a body in here."

"One of the infected?" Chris asked.

"No. Looks dead."

"You think they were attacked by one of the infected?"

"I don't know. I'll let you know when I get down there."

Jade tossed the bag onto the floor. Then she threw her legs over the edge and swung down, keeping a grip on the edge and hanging before letting go. She dropped to a crouched position, then rose and surveyed her surroundings.

She made her way to the body on the floor.

"It's a guy in a suit," she said to Chris. "Looks like he was shot." She kneeled to examine the body briefly. "Name tag says Russell."

"That's the call we heard about from the local police. He must have caught the Doctor down there."

"And he shot him for his efforts," Jade said.

"Well, think about it this way: at least he didn't become one of those infected monsters."

"True."

Jade stood and moved to the ventilation system. Behind a grate was a black cylinder with a screen. She tried to pull the grate away, but it was screwed in. She brushed her fingers across the screws.

"Problem," Jade said.

"What's wrong?" Chris asked.

"I found the device we're looking for. But I need a screwdriver to get to it. It's behind a grate that's screwed into the system."

Jade scoured the room for a tool to unscrew the grate. There was a door behind her, the ventilation system in front of her, and a dead body a few feet away. She rummaged through the pockets of the lifeless body and discovered a wallet, but found nothing useful in it. As she tossed it on the ground, something else caught her eye—the metallic name tag on Russell's shirt. She reached down and, with a quick tug, she yanked it off.

This may work, she thought.

She returned to the grate and placed the corner of the name tag between the screws. It seemed like an eternity until she finally got a grip of the first screw.

She tapped her ear. "Found something to use. Unscrewing the grate now."

"Good," Chris replied. "I'm going to connect you with Stevens on his phone. He's going to walk you through the next steps when you get the grate open."

"Alright," Jade said. "Talk to me, Stevens. What do I do?"

"There's a hand-held device inside the bag you're carrying," Stevens said. "It's yellow and looks like one of those old portable phones from the eighties and nineties. There's a wire attached to it that leads to something that looks like a pipe. You need to get as close to the device as possible, stick that pipe on top of it—or inside, if possible—and determine if it's still emitting anything."

"How do I do that?"

"I already programmed it, so all you have to do is turn it on. The machine will do the rest. Oh, and make sure you bring the device back with you. I want to examine it myself," Stevens said.

"Copy," Jade said. "I'm almost in—one more screw to go."

"Perfect."

Jade had finally unscrewed the last screw. She pulled the grate away and placed it on the floor.

"I'm in," she said. She stared at the black cylinder. Its screen displayed 0:00. There was a small opening at the top of the device. Jade examined it, reaching out to touch it.

This must be where the pathogen was released, she thought.

She unzipped the bag and reached inside, pulling out the device along with the pipe-like apparatus Stevens had mentioned. The device was flat and rectangular, about the size of a tablet. A screen took up most of its bottom half. Directly above it were three switches, with buttons in between them. The top of the device had a hard plastic strip across it.

"What am I looking at here? How do I read this thing?" she asked.

"There should be a switch on it," Stevens said.

Jade ran her hand over the three switches. "Which one? I see three."

"Furthest left."

Jade flipped the switch and the device dinged. Lights on the top lit and she heard a mechanical hum emitting from it. Numbers and symbols flashed on the screen.

"Okay, it's on," she said. "What now?"

"I calibrated it earlier, so all you have to do is turn on the sensor by flipping the right-hand switch, and stick it near the device that was used to distribute the virus."

Jade flipped the rightmost switch and the sensor beeped. She unhooked it and held it over the Doctor's device.

"Anything?" Stevens asked.

"You tell me. I'm holding this metal rod over the device and nothing's happening."

"What do you mean, nothing's happening?" he asked.

Suddenly, the screen beeped.

"Hold on," Jade said. She picked up the device from the floor and looked at it. "Your thing beeped at me and now it says 'negative' with what looks to be an error code."

"Wait—was it a long beep or a short one?"

"A short one."

"Okay, that's a good sign. That means it's not currently releasing anything."

"What if the virus is still in the air?" Jade asked.

"You told me there's an error message. I need to play with it and fix it before we can get it working again."

"Can't I do it from here?" Jade asked.

"Do you know how to debug a mini computer like that? Go through all the prompts and analyze what the error is and fix it?"

"Can't you just walk me through it?"

"It'll be easier if you just bring it back to me. I'll fix it."

"Fine, but you're saying the device isn't emitting anything, right? I don't want to be carrying this thing around while it's still active."

"Based on the short beep you heard, I don't believe it's currently releasing anything," Stevens said.

Jade turned Stevens' machine off and tossed it back inside the duffel bag. She reached into the vent and picked up the canister. It was heavier than she had expected. She placed it gently inside the bag and zipped it up. She slung it over her shoulder.

* * *

"Question," Jade said, over the earpiece. "How am I going to get back to you guys?"

Chris looked wide-eyed as Stevens. "Shit."

"What?" Stevens asked.

"Jade is stuck," he told Stevens. Then he tapped on his ear. "Jade, you definitely can't go back the way you came in. It's flooded with infected."

"I didn't plan on it." Jade said. "I don't see myself getting up there anyway. It's too high to climb back up. Any other suggestions?"

Chris looked along the hallway—he counted four infected wandering around.

He thought about coming down the hallway to get her, but then thought about all the infected still inside the room where Jade was previously. He feared any attempt at saving her would not only endanger himself but put Stevens' and Jade's lives on the line as well.

He tapped his ear. "You're going to have to come down the hallway and shoot your way out. There are currently four of them in the hallway. I'll cover you from here."

"No," Stevens said.

Chris spun around to face him. "I told you, this is *my* mission. *Do not* interfere with the safety of my team."

"But—" Stevens began, but that was all he could say before Chris spoke again to Jade.

"We're going to have to be fast. The moment you step out that door, you need to run. Those gunshots will draw them to you and you need to get past that first room before they come out after you."

***

Jade hesitated, feeling her pulse quicken. She gave a decisive nod. She was ready.

I can do this, she told herself.

She started walking towards the door to the room.

Chris spoke again. "Jade?"

"I'm here," she whispered. She opened the door slowly and to see the four infected Chris had mentioned. "You sure this is going to work?"

"No, I'm not sure."

"Oh, thanks. Just what I needed—uncertainty. I was kinda looking for some confidence here."

"I got your back. Just be quick. Don't start shooting until you have to because once you do, you'll draw them after you," he told her.

"Okay." Jade opened the door wider. "Get ready."

The infected in the hallway were moving aimlessly, seeming distracted by the noises coming from the room containing more of their kind.

Now, she told herself, then darted from the room. With her handgun firmly clutched in her hand, she approached the first infected. The door she had just passed through closed behind her. The noise alerted the infected in the hallway. The first infected Jade approached was a woman. She spun around and her lips were curled with saliva dripping from her mouth.

Jade lowered her head and barreled directly into the woman with fearless determination, sending her crashing against the wall, then tumbling to the ground. She quickly aimed her weapon at another approaching infected, and fired off a shot. It collapsed backwards with a *thud.*

Suddenly, a deafening roar of voices came from the room Jade was passing. She ducked instinctively as a *pop* came from the far end of the hallway. Chris had taken out one of the infected in front of her. It fell to the floor and Jade leaped over the body in her path.

As she passed the broken door from the room she had first entered, a swarm of infected stampeded out towards her. She barely escaped as they reached for her. The first two infected crashed against the wall while a few others shoved their way into the hallway.

"Run!" Chris shouted.

Jade went to target the remaining infected coming at her, but Chris quickly fired another two shots, sending them tumbling towards her. With quick reflexes, she leaped over the bodies, but her foot became tangled in a flailing limb, sending her off balance and stumbling.

The tumbling corpse was an unstoppable force, crashing into the other infected and causing a domino effect that brought down those emerging from the room.

Jade rolled over quickly and got back to her feet, but then something stopped her from moving forward—a hand. One of the infected had taken a hold of her foot.

Acting on instinct, Jade went for her gun. Her pulse quickened as she realized she had dropped it when she fell, and it now lay a few feet away. She lashed out with her free leg to kick the infected in the face. Its head snapped back, but it still held tightly on to her leg.

Some of the infected were only a few feet away. Jade had to get free, fast. She kicked the infected in the face a second time, but it still held on firmly, growing angrier with each kick. Jade kicked it again, finally freeing herself, then she surged forward, away from the infected on the floor. She bent over and snatched her gun before sprinting towards Chris and Stevens at the end of the hallway.

Chris flicked his hand, in a gesture for Jade to move out of the way. As she pressed up against the wall, Chris fired his weapon multiple times, sending more of the infected crashing down.

"Let's go!" Chris exclaimed.

Jade sprinted up the stairs first, followed by Stevens. Chris looked around the corner one last time, fired his gun, then headed upstairs.

| 10 |

After the fifth game of I-spy, Myles finally told Caroline he'd had enough.

"I'll play with you, little girl," Emily yelled up to Caroline.

Caroline looked over the railing to see Emily staring up at her. She beamed with excitement—a smile from ear to ear. "Yay!"

Emily couldn't help but smile at Caroline's simple excitement, a feeling that dug deep within her—lifting her mood and providing a much needed distraction from the dangers surrounding them.

"You turning into a nerd, too?" Frank asked.

"Actually, I take pride in being a nerd. I play video games. I read books."

She took a few steps closer to Frank.

"Are you nervous around nerds?" she asked.

He looked her up and down. "Not cute ones."

"Gross," Emily said, flipping her hair back as she spun away from him.

James pointed to Emily and smirked. "You're blushing."

Emily scowled at James, and waved dismissively.

"Aww," Frank said. "Did I make you blush?"

Emily ignored him and looked back up at Caroline, who was leaning on the railing. "Are you ready to play?"

Gunshots went off in the distance.

Everyone's heads jerked up.

"You hear that?" Frank asked.

More gunshots.

"Stay here," Frank said.

"Not like I can go anywhere," Myles said.

"Wait, what? Where are you going?" Emily shouted as Frank jogged away.

***

Frank made his way into the hallway as Jade came rushing out of a doorway.

"Get something to hold this door shut!" she yelled.

Frank hesitated. "What?"

"I need something to hold this door shut. Now!"

Stevens burst from the basement in a frenzied hurry. Gunfire echoed from the stairwell behind him.

"Chris!" Jade yelled down the stairs. "Come on!"

Chris sprinted up the stairs, taking two at a time. He had a decent lead on the infected, but he knew it wouldn't last long.

He climbed to the last stair and made it out of the basement. Jade slammed the door shut. Chris took out his keys locked the door.

"Frank, you got anything for this door?" Jade said.

Frank ran towards the door, placing a trash can in front of it.

Jade looked at him, dumbfounded. "*That's* what you got?"

"Oh, *I'm sorry,*" Frank said sarcastically. "This empty hallway doesn't have all the resources you require at the snap of a finger."

"That's not going to hold them," Chris said. "We need to go now."

The banging on the door began. It rattled as the infected pounded on it from the other side. The door started to push outward due to the weight pressing against it.

Myles' voice came over the earpiece. "Guys, we have a problem."

Jade, Frank, Chris, and Stevens started running through the hallways, back to the lobby.

"Yes, we know," Frank said. "I'm with Chris and the others now. A group of these infected will be on us shortly. Get ready. They'll be coming our way."

"What? No," Myles said. "Emily and James said they heard footsteps and growling from down the hallway. I don't think we're speaking of the same group of infected."

"More of them?" Chris butted in. "We're running from another group of them right now."

"I don't know—maybe?" Myles replied. "They must have heard you guys."

Chris and the rest of the team sprinted into the lobby to find Emily and James positioning a table underneath the balcony. Emily climbed on top of it, and James tossed her a chair, which she caught and placed on the table to climb on. As she reached up and grabbed the bottom of the balcony, Myles and Ellen leaned over to grab her arms and help her up. Next, James climbed on the table, following Emily up to the balcony.

"Guys, head up there," Chris said. "We need to get to higher ground to stay safe."

"Don't have to tell me twice," Stevens said. He moved quickly towards the table and waited for James to finish his ascent.

A loud cracking sound came from the hallway.

"Sounds like they're out," Jade said. "That trashcan worked wonders."

"Shut up," Frank said.

"Get ready," Chris said.

All three of them aimed their weapons into the depths of the hallway, preparing themselves for what was coming.

The first infected turned the corner and made its way into view. Jade, Chris, and Frank opened fire, dropping the one infected instantly. Three more appeared and they opened fire again. Two of the infected didn't make it more than a few steps along the hallway before being taken down, but one made it into the lobby before it died. A handful more came running down the hallway.

"We can't hold them all off with the limited ammo we have," Chris said, firing another few shots.

"What's the plan, then?" Jade asked.

Chris turned to see Stevens climbing over the railing. He pointed and shouted back to Frank and Jade. "Up there. We have to move."

As more infected charged towards them, another herd of infected, at least twenty strong, began tailing the first group.

"We have to get up that balcony. *Now*!" Chris shouted. "Frank, go. Give us cover from above."

Frank nodded. He planted a foot on the table, stepped onto the chair, and jumped up to grab onto the railing. Stevens and Myles reached out to pull him up over the railing.

Chris and Jade kept firing, taking out multiple infected, but they kept coming. Chris knew there must have been an end to this herd of infected, but he couldn't see it.

"Anytime now, Frank!" Chris shouted.

Frank climbed over the railing and turned to aim his gun below.

Chris shot an infected to his right. One got into the lobby and charged to his left. As Chris went to turn, a shot rang out, and the infected dropped beside him, splattering droplets of blood on Chris's arm. He looked above him and saw Frank, waving to him.

Jade and Chris made their way to the table, continuing to shoot at the infected heading towards them.

"Jade, go!" Chris shouted. In the split second it had taken to turn and speak to her, multiple infected had invaded their space and were now up close and personal with them.

"I don't have a shot!" Frank yelled to Chris.

Chris shot one of the infected that was directly in front of him.

Jade jumped on the table and aimed down, firing her weapon around Chris to take out the infected close to him as he made his way onto the table.

With a sudden jolt, Jade was pulled backwards. One of the infected had hold of the duffel bag slung on her shoulder. Before it could drag her off the table, Chris reached out and caught her hand, keeping her on her feet, then fired his weapon at the infected. As it fell, it kept a tight grip on the duffel bag, snapping the strap on Jade's shoulder.

"Shit, the bag!" Jade yelled.

"Forget it. We'll get it later," Chris told her. "Get up there."

He turned and fired a few more shots until his handgun was out of ammunition. He turned to see Jade being safely pulled over the railing. Chris stood on the chair and went to jump, but his escape was thwarted as an infected pulled on his leg. He went to kick it, but the infected pulled harder, making him lose his balance and fall off the chair, crashing onto the table.

"Chris!" Jade yelled.

Chris stared up at Jade who was leaning over the railing. His vision was blurred. He laid there for a moment. His breathing was weak. He blinked slowly. Everything was silent. Jade was mouthing something, but he couldn't make it out. He looked around and suddenly he snapped out of his trance.

His vision came into focus. The terrifying noises of the monsters once again echoed around him.

Chris got to his feet and went to step on the chair, but then an infected came rushing at him. He threw his gun at its head.

It bounced off, knocking the infected to the ground—which gave Chris all the time he needed.

He stepped onto the chair and jumped up to the railing. Myles and Frank leaned over the ledge and began pulling him up, just as an infected grabbed a hold of Chris's foot.

As the infected held onto Chris, the extra weight started to pull him down, making Frank and Myles lose their balance slightly. Chris's heart was already beating out of his chest. The fear of dying by one of those things was something he wanted no part of, but he couldn't help but be terrified of the thought of it. His grip on his team above started to slip.

Jade leaned over the edge.

"Get the hell off of him!" she shouted, firing her weapon at the infected's head. It lost its grip and fell from the table, along with the chair.

Frank and Myles pulled Chris over the railing, and the three of them collapsed in a heap.

"You okay?" Jade asked.

Chris nodded. "Everyone else okay up here?"

The response was a collective "Yeah."

Chris stood up and joined Frank to look over the railing.

"I count thirteen," Frank said.

"Can we just shoot them all from up here and then go back down?" Myles asked.

"Sure. Do you have another magazine for me?" Frank said. "Because I have almost no ammo left."

"And I'm out," Chris said.

"I'm on my last magazine too," Jade said.

"Then to answer your question, Myles," Frank said, "yes, we can shoot them all from up here. But will we get a kill shot with each one? Maybe, but maybe not. So, I'd kind of like to save the ammo for now."

"Frank's right," Chris said. "We need to conserve our ammunition. We don't know what else may happen."

"Oh, I enjoy hearing that," Frank said. "Say 'I'm right' again."

"Shut up, Frank," Jade said.

Stevens looked around, frantic. "Jade, where's the device?"

She pointed over the railing at the black duffel bag on the lobby floor. "Right there."

"We need to get it back. That's how we can tell if the infection is still present in the air," Stevens said.

"And how do you expect us to get it, Doc?" Frank asked. He put an arm around Stevens' shoulders and escorted him to the railing to show him the infected below. "Would you like to go down there and get it?"

Stevens shuddered.

"Thought not," Frank said, releasing him.

"Umm... Chris?" Myles said.

"What?" Chris asked.

"Your leg."

Chris looked down and saw a tear in his suit.

| 11 |

A wave of nausea flowed through Chris. Had he been infected?

He bent over and rubbed his hand over the tear in his suit. It was from his shin down to his left foot, exposing his clothing and skin underneath. He stuck his hand inside and felt the fabric of his pants.

Chris lifted his gaze to meet the eyes of those around him. He swallowed hard. The nausea had disappeared, but it was immediately replaced by anxiety as he felt himself tense in alarm. He had to remain calm. He couldn't let his team know he was suddenly fearful for his life. He didn't want to become one of those *things.*

Those infected *things.*

Those drooling, growling, disgusting *things.*

That wasn't how he wanted his life to end.

He glanced nervously around the room. Everyone was focused intently on him. Had they noticed a change he couldn't see? He didn't feel any different. Were they expecting him to turn into one of those infected monsters?

He held up his hands. "Guys, let's not panic here."

"Maybe we can patch it up," Jade said.

Chris shook his head. "It's too late at this point. If the virus is in the air, we have to assume I'm already exposed."

Jade turned to Stevens. "There has to be something we can do, right?"

"I'm sorry. If his suit is compromised, there's nothing we can do. If the virus is still active and the air has gotten inside, then he's been exposed."

"There has to be another way to save him," Myles said.

"There is," Stevens said. He turned and looked over the railing. "We need that device. I can figure out if the virus is still active in the air if I can get the equipment in that bag."

"Doc, not sure if you overheard the conversation we just had when you were literally a foot away," Frank said. "But we're low on ammo. And there's an army of them down there. There ain't no way we're going down there right now."

"Even if it means knowing if your commander is infected or not?" Stevens asked. "If he's infected, maybe we can find a way to reverse the infection. If he's not, wouldn't that give you guys," Stevens then looked at Chris, "especially you, a peace of mind knowing that you're okay?"

"No offense. But how will knowing if the virus is still in the air help if Chris is infected?" Frank asked.

"It won't," Stevens said. "But wouldn't you like to know if your commander is going turn into one of those things around us?"

They all stood silent for a moment.

"But like I said," Stevens said, "maybe there's a way to reverse it."

Jade looked over the edge. "So, how do we get down there?"

"We make a distraction," Emily said.

Everyone looked at her, confused at her joining in the conversation unexpectedly.

She continued, "I used to distract my parents when I wanted to sneak out of my house as a teenager. I'd pick a fight with my little sister. She'd get angry and upset, and my parents would comfort her and punish me. I'd pretend to get angry and lock myself in my room. Then I'd sneak out while they were distracted taking care of her." Emily looked around at everyone, seemingly reading everyone's faces. "I know. I was a bitch to her, but it worked. If you can figure out a way to distract those things down there then you should be in the clear, right?"

Jade was the first to speak up.

"She may have a point. If we can lure them away from the lobby somehow, we could get down there and retrieve the bag."

"How?" Frank asked.

"Bait," Myles said.

"I'm sorry, did you just say what I think you did?" Frank said.

"If one of us goes down there and lures them into the hallway, they'll follow. It'll clear out the lobby and we can take down any stragglers," Chris said. "It's a good idea."

"And which one of you idiots is going to get yourself killed running from those things?" Frank asked.

Chris raised his hand. "I'll go. If I'm infected, it doesn't matter if they get me, right?"

"But we don't know if you're infected," Jade said.

"What about them?" Chris pointed to Emily, James, Ellen, and her daughter. "We don't know if they're infected or not either. It's my job to help. I'm going down there."

"Then I'm going with you," Jade said.

"Good. You two crazies can go for a game of tag with those monsters down there," Frank said.

"You're staying here, Jade," Chris said.

"Like hell I am," she replied. "I'm coming along to make sure it's not a suicide mission."

Chris knew that once Jade got an idea in her mind, it was hard to convince her otherwise. Even using his rank and ordering her to stay wouldn't work. She'd come with him, whether or not he liked it.

"Fine. Jade and I will go down there and lure them away. Myles—when the coast is clear, you'll climb down and grab the bag and get your ass back up here."

"Wait, why do *I* have to go down there?"

"Because I'm the better shot, dumbass," Frank said. "I need to protect your ass from above."

"Shit," Myles said, realizing Frank was right.

"Is there anything I can do to help?" Ellen asked.

Chris placed a hand on her shoulder. "You can take care of that daughter of yours. Keep her safe up here."

Chris walked over to Myles. "Pull up the schematics for this place. I need to know exactly where we're leading these things to when Jade and I get down there."

"On it," Myles said, and pulled out his phone, swiping at its screen.

"Jade, come with me," Chris said.

The pair peered over the railing. Chris unzipped the top of his hazmat suit and started to take it off.

"Stop. What are you doing?" Jade asked.

He tossed the top portion of his hazmat suit on the ground. He brushed a hand through his salt and pepper hair.

He sighed. "That feels so much better now."

"But your suit..."

"I'm already exposed, remember?" Chris reminded her. "What does it matter now if I'm wearing it or not?"

Jade's somber look worried Chris. He knew she cared. He had to distract her.

He pointed to the hallway. "There. That's where we're going. Those things are going to follow us. And they're fast. We need to know where we're going before we get in there."

"Here, boss," Myles said, handing his phone to Chris, as well as his handgun. "You'll need this."

"Thank you." Chris stuck the gun in his holster, then held the phone so that both he and Jade could see it. He pointed to the screen. "This is where we are now. Once we go down that hallway, we're going to go past the elevators." He scrolled along the hall. "Here. At the end of the hallway, we're going left. There's the staircase at the end. We take that upstairs."

"What if they keep following us upstairs?" Jade asked.

Chris hesitated. "We'll just keep moving."

"That doesn't sound like the confident Chris Hoffman I know," Jade said.

Chris wanted to protect her. He wanted to protect everyone. He wished he had more of a plan, but he was out of ideas. He had never expected to fall into a situation like this. He knew he may not make it out of this hotel, but he wanted to make sure Jade and the others did.

He turned and handed the phone back to Myles.

"Everyone ready?" Chris asked.

They all nodded in agreement.

"Good. Let's go."

| 12 |

Chris watched as the group of monsters lurked below him. His pulse raced and adrenaline flooded through his body. He reminded himself that he had been through worse situations than this.

Have I? he thought.

He shook the thought away and turned to Jade.

"You ready?" he asked.

She nodded.

Chris picked up the top part of his hazmat suit, then tossed it over the ledge as far as he could towards the front door. As the suit made its way to the floor, the infected ran towards it, giving Chris and Jade their opportunity.

Chris swung himself over the ledge and slid down the railing before letting go, landing softly on his toes, careful not to make much noise. He glanced at the infected pouncing on his hazmat suit. He knew he had only seconds left. He looked up at Jade and waved for her to follow before it was too late.

Jade copied Chris's technique of getting down. As she was dangling from the bottom of the railing, a loud growl came from the front of the lobby.

The infected had spotted them.

"Jade, hurry," Chris said.

She dropped to the floor, and Chris pulled her to her feet. Jade took out her handgun and fired a single shot at the leading infected. It was a direct shot to its head. Chris and Jade had already turned and headed towards the hallway before the deceased infected struck the floor. They disappeared down the hallway, the infected not far behind them.

***

"It worked," Emily said.

"Hopefully they're okay down there," Myles said.

Frank patted him on the back. "Alright, hotshot. You're up."

Myles sighed. "Alright. Let's get this over with."

"Here," Frank said, "take my handgun—just in case."

"Just in case of what?" Myles said.

"Well, you gave yours away to Chris, you idiot. What do you have to protect yourself?"

Myles took the handgun and slid it into his holster, realizing Frank was right. "Thank you."

He stood by the railing and looked down. Blood pooled across the tiled floor. Debris and dead infected lay all around. Myles glanced back at Frank, who waved him on. Emily and James stood side by side, observing. Ellen and Caroline sat further away, probably playing another game of I-spy. Myles wished he was doing that instead.

Here goes nothing.

He climbed over the railing and slid down gently until he held onto the bottom of the posts, his legs dangling. He let go and dropped to the floor. He landed hard and stumbled to the floor.

"Dammit," he said.

"What's wrong?" Frank asked.

Myles sat and brought his hands to his ankle. "I think I twisted my ankle."

"Can you walk?" Stevens asked.

Myles nodded. "Yeah, I'll be good."

He looked around and felt relieved knowing the area was empty. Slowly, Myles climbed to his feet and limped to the duffel bag a few feet away. He picked it up and tossed it over his shoulder.

Someone screamed from above.

Myles looked up at the railing above him.

A gunshot.

What the hell is happening?

More screaming.

"Guys?" Myles said.

"Shit, shit, shit..." he heard Frank say from above.

"What the hell is going on up there?" Myles asked again.

Noises came from the hallway to his right.

The infected were coming back.

"Guys? I need some help down here," Myles said.

He heard a chaotic symphony of sounds from above—the rushed footsteps, muffled voices and snippets of distant conversation.

"Hello?" he said again. "Help!"

The noises grew louder from the hallway.

Myles pulled out his handgun and prepared himself.

***

Chris and Jade sprinted along the hallway and turned the corner towards the staircase. Despite their head start, Chris was beginning to worry that the infected would catch up with them soon.

"We have to get through that door and get it shut quick," Chris said, pointing at the door at the end of the hallway.

Chris reached the door first and swung it open. He waved Jade through. "Come on," he said. He slammed the door shut behind her. Jade picked up a broomstick and slid it between the door handle and the wall.

"This should slow them down," she said.

Chris nodded. "Hopefully."

They hurried to the stairs, and began to make their way up.

Banging on the door below jolted them to a standstill. The door yanked but was prevented from opening by the broom.

"That won't hold them for long," Chris said.

They continued to the second floor. As they reached it, a loud snap of splintering wood echoed downstairs. The infected had made their way into the staircase.

When Chris and Jade emerged onto the second floor, they headed to the first hotel room they encountered.

"You think we're safe in here?" Jade asked.

Before Chris could respond, he heard a faint gunshot.

They looked at each other and waited.

"Only one," Jade said.

Chris shrugged. He placed his finger on his ear, "Guys, come in. Everyone okay?"

No answer.

Footsteps came from within the room. Jade reached for the light switch, revealing an infected. It ran towards them.

Chris pushed Jade aside, putting her out of harm's way. She fell to the floor next to the bed. Chris went to grab his handgun, but the overweight infected man, wearing jeans and a blue hoodie, got to him first. He lost his grip, and the gun fell to the floor. The infected toppled him over and pinned him beneath its massive weight.

Jade jumped to her feet and grabbed the lamp next to the bed. She ripped the cord from the wall and with a powerful swing, brought the lamp crashing down on the head of the infected. The bulb exploded and shattered as it hit its mark—but this only seemed to fuel the monster's rage further. It continued to attack Chris until Jade used the cord and wrapped it around the infected's neck. She tugged violently on the cord and lifted the infected away from Chris, trying to suffocate it.

Chris reached behind him, pulled one of the drawers out from the dresser and smashed it into the infected's head—repeatedly.

Finally, the infected fell to the ground and went limp.

Jade released her grip on the cord around its neck.

"Is it dead?" she asked.

Chris bent down to pick up his gun. "Not sure. But not sticking around to find out."

He made his way over to the door and placed his ear against it.

"Anything?" she asked.

"I don't hear anything," he whispered. "Maybe that other gunshot distracted them."

Cautiously, he cracked the door open just enough to see outside. At first glance, he saw nothing, but as he opened it further, his gaze settled upon several infected wandering at the far end of the hallway.

"We should be good," he said as he turned back to Jade, but then suddenly aimed his gun in Jade's direction.

"Watch out!" he yelled and fired his weapon.

The infected had climbed to its feet and was about to attack Jade —but now it was dead.

"We gotta go," Chris said.

"Yeah, that's going to get their attention," Jade said.

Chris swung the door open and looked in the direction where the infected had been. They had already started towards them.

"This way," Chris said, and started heading back towards the stairs. Chris opened the door to the staircase and was greeted by an infected standing next to the banister. It turned and growled at them. Chris charged forward and sent the monster flying over the railing with a powerful push, tumbling to the first floor with flailing limbs as its arms and legs hit a railing on the way down.

Chris waved Jade on, and the two of them climbed the stairs.

***

Myles pulled the hammer back and aimed his gun along the dark hallway. The noises became louder.

What's happening above me, and why aren't they responding?

Did an infected get up there?

The first infected made an appearance, rushing towards him. He fired his weapon, hitting the infected in the chest. It stumbled for a moment but continued towards Myles. He fired two more times. His second shot missed, but the third shot hit the infected in the leg, making it stumble, but it kept on coming. Myles' hands trembled as the infected made its way closer to him. He fired once more. He had sworn he'd missed, but the infected's head jolted back and fell to the floor.

"Aim for the head, dummy," Frank yelled down to him from the lounge area. "Instant kill."

"Where the hell have you been?" Myles asked.

Frank pointed to the hallway. "Less talk, more getting your ass back up here. Set that chair on the table again and climb up. I'll cover you until we can pull you back up."

Myles stared down at the dead infected on top of the chair. He didn't want to touch one of those things. What if it wasn't dead? What if it woke up and attacked him?

Fear jolted him into action as the menacing growls and heavy footsteps grew closer.

He had to move.

With a quick pull, he released the chair from underneath one of the infected corpses. He placed it on the table and climbed up.

Two shots came from above.

"Would you hurry up already…" Frank said.

Frank fired another shot, which startled Myles and almost made him lose his balance. He stood upon the chair and jumped, grabbing onto the railing.

It wasn't the best grip, though. He started to slip. The weight of the bag on his bag on his shoulder didn't help.

His hand was about to slip off entirely when a hand grabbed him. Myles looked up to see Frank holding onto him.

"Can someone help me here, please?" Frank pleaded.

Emily rushed over and reached for Myles's other arm. Together, they brought Myles up a bit more until he could finally get a footing on the ledge. He climbed over the banister, swung his feet over, and landed on the floor.

He had made it.

He laid on his back and let out the biggest sigh of relief.

He hoped the adrenaline would subside within his body at some point soon. It was making him feel ill.

A hand fell beside him. Myles noticed Frank standing over him. He took his hand and was helped up.

"What the hell, man?" Myles said. "Why was I left down there like that? What happened up here?"

Frank sidestepped to reveal two bodies on the floor.

Myles glanced at Frank, then back at the two bodies.

"Oh no," he said.

Emily's friend—James—was lying face down in a pool of his own blood.

The other body was Stevens.

| 13 |

Chris and Jade sprinted up the third flight of stairs, escaping the horde of infected behind them. As they approached the door to the fourth floor, it opened abruptly and an infected stumbled out of the darkness. Jade instinctively raised her weapon to meet it—two shots later, the infected crumpled to the floor in front of them.

They jumped over the body and continued up to the roof. With a determined push, Chris dropped his shoulder and blasted through the door, bursting onto the rooftop. Jade slammed the door behind her and braced herself for what seemed like an inevitable attack at any second from the infected following behind them.

Chris began searching for anything to help them barricade door.

Suddenly, Jade was shoved forward and bounced off the door.

"Chris! Hurry!" she yelled.

She dug her feet into the rooftop as best she could, gritting her teeth as she fought against the infected trying to force the door open. But, despite her efforts, it wasn't working. She was slowly being pushed forward.

Chris ran towards a pile of junk, but after tossing a few things aside, he concluded there was nothing useful.

"Chris!"

He turned to see Jade struggling. He needed to find something, fast.

He spotted something sticking up behind a pipe. A small ladder, but heavy enough to do some damage to these monsters.

He picked it up and ran back to the door, holding the legs of the ladder in front of him.

"Open the door!" he yelled.

Jade was clearly confused, but she followed orders as Chris wasn't slowing down.

When she opened the door, three infected stumbled onto the rooftop. Another six stood behind them. Chris attacked them with the ladder, ramming the infected and sending them tumbling down the stairs like bowling pins.

"Close it!" Chris yelled as he jumped out of the way.

Jade slammed the door shut at the same time Chris took his first shot at one of the three infected who made their way back to their feet. His accurate headshot made the infected man's baseball hat fall off his head.

The other two stood up.

Chris took another shot at the infected closest to him, but hit him in the chest. The infected man's white T-shirt became stained in blood and he stumbled backwards slightly. As Chris went to take another shot, the other infected ran into him, knocking the gun out of his hand.

Jade took out her gun and fired a shot at the infected woman. The woman's frizzy brown hair blew in the wind as the bullet Jade had just fired missed its mark, but it got the infected's attention. Chris seized on the opportunity, grabbing the monster's head and slamming it against the door repeatedly until her body was lifeless.

Jade fired a final shot at the remaining infected and dropped it with a head shot.

Banging came from the stairwell.

The infected were on their way back up.

"Chris—here."

Jade had picked up Chris's gun and tossed it to him. He caught it just as the door opened, and fired a shot immediately, dropping the first infected.

The remaining infected plowed through, running towards Chris. He fired another shot frantically and then turned to run. The infected continued their pursuit.

Jade took aim and fired her weapon—hitting one of the infected in its shoulder. Despite being jolted back by the force, it continued forward. She fired one last time before turning to run, this time landing a fatal blow to its head.

Chris and Jade jumped over a pipe to put some distance between them and the infected.

"What's your count?" Chris asked.

Jade ejected her magazine and counted the bullets. "Two. You?"

"One bullet left," he said. They ran around an air duct and crouched, trying to stay hidden. "Pick your shot carefully."

Jade nodded.

Chris took a look above the vent. "Here they come. Stay here. I'm going to lead them away. Take your shots as they run by." He stood up and sprinted away from Jade.

The infected grew louder as they approached Jade's hiding spot. The first infected ran by in a black and white tracksuit, her ponytail flapping behind her. Then came the second infected, a man dressed in khakis and a black sweater. When the third ran by, she aimed and fired. The infected stopped in his tracks and turned to face Jade, staring back at her with black aviator glasses.

"Dammit," she said. She fired again. The infected's head snapped backwards and it fell onto the rooftop. His glasses fell off his head and bounced to Jade's feet. The fourth infected turned the corner and headed for her.

Chris raced across the rooftop, searching frantically for anything to help him fend off the pursuing infected. He glanced over his shoulder to keep track of how much ground was between him and the infected.

These things are fast, he thought.

He had put some more space between them.

He used his momentum to lift his legs and slide over a ledge. He landed effortlessly back on his feet and kept running.

He looked over his shoulder again and saw the infected pause at the ledge and struggle to pass it. This was his opportunity. He stopped and aimed his gun at one of them.

He fired his last bullet.

The infected in the track suit that had already climbed over the ledge fell backwards onto the roof. The other infected in the black sweater kept climbing over and making his way towards Chris.

***

Jade sprinted away from the infected that had begun to chase her. The chains on the infected man's leather jacket jingled as he ran. His shaved head and scruffy face made him appear more intimidating than he already was.

As she fled, a wave of fear coursed through her veins. The flavor of adrenaline was strong in her mouth, bitter like the taste of blood. With her empty gun in hand and no plan of escape, she couldn't believe the situation she had found herself in—running from a monster.

She had always believed monsters didn't exist. It wasn't until this team formed that she had been proven wrong. Monsters did exist. But the *actual* monster was the one who developed the virus that created these things—the Doctor. She hoped she'd live long enough to hunt this guy down. She didn't want to end up like one of these infected things.

Something hit her leg, and she lost her balance, sliding on the rooftop. She was only a few feet from the ledge.

Quickly, she rolled onto her back and saw the infected was on the ground too. He raised himself onto all fours and started crawling frantically towards her.

Jade moved backwards, but stopped as her hand slid off the edge of the roof. She glanced over, her heart pounding in her chest at the sight below—the roof was much higher than she had expected.

She leapt to her feet and moved away from the ledge before unleashing a mighty kick at the face of the infected crawling towards her. She went to run but was held back by a firm grip on her ankle. She laid into the infected with another kick to its face.

It was as if the monster felt no pain. Despite Jade's kicking, he kept coming.

Abruptly, it released Jade's ankle as it was dragged away.

Jade spotted Chris pulling at the infected's feet. It desperately attempted to roll over and launch an attack at Chris. He released the infected's legs and pounced on it with an unrelenting flurry of punches.

"Chris, watch out!" Jade yelled as the other infected in the black sweater ran around the corner and collided with Chris.

He tumbled off the infected and readied himself for the attacking monster. It leapt towards him, but Chris used his hands and feet to block the attack, throwing the infected off balance.

After a few steps, it regained its footing and continued rushing towards Jade. He barreled into her and shoved her backwards, pushing her towards the edge. The weight and momentum continued pushing her backwards, and as she lost her balance.

Jade slipped off the ledge, screaming.

***

"Jade!" Chris yelled, extending his hand, as if it would make a difference from over ten feet away.

He watched as both Jade and the infected disappeared from the roof. Seconds later, a faint *boom* came from below.

Chris's eyes widened with alarm. He was rigid with fear as a wave of butterflies rose from his stomach. He was terrified to look over the edge. He didn't want to see his team member splattered on the pavement below.

He began to climb to his feet, but the infected beat him to it and jumped on his back. Chris threw an elbow in its face which made the chains jingle on the infected's jacket, but it didn't loosen its grip. He threw another one and heard a crack. The infected finally lost its grip and Chris could slide free.

"Chris, help!"

It was Jade's voice.

The distraction was what the infected had needed. It attacked Chris again and knocked him to the rooftop, then jumped on top of him, screaming in his face. Blood dripped from the infected and onto Chris's neck and shirt. It tried to bite Chris but he managed to stay out of reach of its jaws.

Chris struggled to kick the infected off of him as it pulled its arm back for a punch. He managed to narrowly dodge each successive onslaught.

"Help!" Jade's voice echoed again.

Chris began balling his hands into fists. His nails dug into the palms of his hands. His muscles tightened. The rush of adrenaline made it hard for him to think. The only thing on his mind was getting to Jade.

The infected roared in Chris's face.

Its pupils and irises were black. The white that had once surrounded the iris was now red. Its eyes were full of rage.

"Get the hell off of me!" Chris barked.

He used all the strength he had left to knock the infected away. It rolled to his right and shot back to its feet almost instantly. It leaned forward, stretching its arms out, ready to attack.

It took one step before coming to a halt.

A gunshot came from somewhere on the roof.

Who fired that? Chris thought.

The infected turned in the noise's direction. It snarled at its attacker's direction before two more gunshots rang out. The infected fell and remained motionless.

Chris raised his head to see Officer Cohen standing beside the fire escape.

Realizing that the threat was eliminated, Chris jumped to his feet and raced to the edge of the roof.

Jade was hanging on to the gutter.

He couldn't believe it. She was really alive. Relief flushed over him.

Chris extended his hand for her to take. They connected and locked fingers. He had a good grip on her, but pulling her up with one hand was a daunting task given the pain he was experiencing.

"Officer Cohen—a little help?" he asked.

A moment later, another hand reached down and grabbed Jade's other arm. Together, Chris and Officer Cohen pulled Jade over the edge of the rooftop. Chris collapsed, lying on his back and staring up at the night sky.

"Are we done with this yet?" he asked.

"What's going on up here?" Officer Cohen asked.

Chris looked up at Officer Cohen and said, "Those infected things attacked us. We lured a few of them up here, but we're out of ammo. Anyway, long story short—thank you for your help back there."

"Sure. Anytime," Officer Cohen said. "How come you don't have your hazmat suit on anymore?"

Chris looked down only now remembering he wasn't wearing it. "Oh yeah. It was damaged earlier, and I took it off. No point in wearing it anymore, right?"

Officer Cohen nodded.

"Thank you for the save," Jade said.

"Of course," Officer Cohen said. "When I saw that body fall off the roof, I knew something was happening. Then I saw someone hanging off the edge and I climbed up the fire escape to help."

"Chris," Jade said, "do you think him being up here puts him at any risk for the virus?"

"I mean, we are outdoors. The virus was released inside the building. I'd say you're safe," Chris said. "Speaking of being safe, anyone hear from the guys inside?"

Jade shook her head.

"Who?" Officer Cohen asked.

Chris ignored his question and put a finger to his ear. "Frank, come in."

"Good to hear from you," Frank replied. "You and Jade alright?"

Chris looked at Jade, thankful she was okay. "We're good. Officer Cohen is up here with us."

"Up where? And who's that?" Frank responded.

"We're on the roof. And Officer Cohen is the officer I spoke with before we entered the building."

"Why the hell are you on the roof?"

"We kept climbing the stairs, and this was the last place to go to escape."

Frank didn't respond.

"Frank? You there?" Chris asked.

"Yeah, sorry. Just trying to figure out how to tell you Stevens is dead."

"Wait. What? Stevens is dead?"

"Damn. I guess I just blurted it out."

"What the hell happened?" Chris asked.

"Still trying to figure that out. The guy who was here with us, James, suddenly turned into one of those things and attacked Stevens. By the time we noticed, it was too late. It happened so fast."

Chris put his head in his hands. Death surrounded him. His heart sank with the news of Stevens's death. He was a friend. Someone he had just spoken to moments ago. The last few times he had with Stevens he was yelling at him. Guilt flooded inside of him. But he took a deep breath and pushed aside his heartache. There'd be time to grieve his loss later. He had to continue the mission.

"Chris?" Frank said.

Chris picked his head up. He noticed Jade staring at him.

"You okay, boss?" she asked.

He nodded, then stood up and stretched out his aching muscles.

"Did you get the device?" he asked Frank.

"Yeah, Myles got it," Frank replied.

"Good. Was Stevens able to read it before..." Chris paused, unwilling to say the words. "...before he died?"

"No," Frank said. "I'm sorry, Chris."

Chris closed his eyes and shook his head.

"You need to call the department and get someone to explain to you how to interpret the device and fix the error message Stevens spoke of. I don't care who you call, but don't stop until you reach someone who can get that device read for you."

"Copy," Frank said.

* * *

"What did he say?" Ellen asked.

"He said to hold tight until we figure out how to read this thing," Frank said.

"You calling, or am I?" Myles asked.

"You call. You're the tech guy. You know how to speak their lingo," Frank replied.

Myles returned Frank's handgun to him, then pulled out his phone and started scrolling through his contacts as he moved away.

"Are Jade and the other gentleman okay?" Ellen asked.

Frank nodded.

Ellen turned to see Emily rocking in the corner, her knees tucked to her chest and her arms wrapped around them.

"What about her?" Ellen asked.

"I'll go talk to her," he said.

Frank made his way over to Emily, taking a comfortable seat beside her. He rested his head against the wall for a moment before turning to face her. Then he looked away and said, "I lost my best friend when I was about ten years old. He was my neighbor—lived three houses down. We used to play outside all the time. It didn't matter what the weather was. It could be pouring rain, one hundred degrees, or a blizzard, we were outside. One day—or rather one evening—we were playing flashlight tag with a few other friends. A drunk driver came speeding down the road that night."

He registered her turning to face him.

"My friend—Ezra—was running across the street. Everyone knew to drive slow in our neighborhood because all the parents knew the kids were always outside playing." Frank shook his head. "Not this guy, though. Just flew down the street like he was on the highway. I think the police said he was going almost sixty miles per hour. They said Ezra died on impact."

"I'm sorry," Emily said.

"It's okay," Frank replied. "You ever see someone hit by a car going sixty miles per hour?"

She shook her head.

"You ever see a deer on the side of a highway? All the blood and pieces of it lying around?"

"Eww."

"Yes. Eww. And you know what I think of every time I see the mayhem we left behind here? All that blood? The dead bodies, either killed by us or ripped apart by those infected things?" He paused. "I think of my friend. I see him when I look around here."

Emily wiped her tears away. "It doesn't seem to bother you, though."

"Because the mission is more important than a distant memory. Getting out of here alive is more important. Keeping you guys safe is more important. You need to focus on what you can do. Deal with your feelings and thoughts after you get out of here—*alive*."

She started to cry again.

"How do you push everything aside, then? How do you forget about it?"

"You don't," he said. He pushed himself up to a standing position. "You're human. Some handle death better than others, but you'll always feel something. You just get good at focusing on other things. Like right now—getting out of here."

He reached down and offered his hand.

She looked at it, then up at him. She took his hand, and he helped her stand.

Noises came from the hallway. Banging in the distance.

Frank let go of Emily's hand and he made his way to the door, pressing his ear against it, and listened.

"God dammit. Will we ever get a break?" he said.

Myles looked at him. "What's wrong?"

Frank backed away from the door.

"They're getting through the barricade."

| 14 |

"So, what's the plan now?" Jade asked.

Chris sat in silence for a moment. His mind was running all over the place. He rubbed his neck gently, trying to figure out a plan.

"We have no ammo," he finally said. "We also have no idea if I'm infected or not."

"I can lend you some guns if you need to get back inside," Officer Cohen interrupted.

"Yes!" Jade said. "You can do that for us?"

"Yeah. I'll be right back."

"Thank you," Chris said.

Officer Cohen headed back towards the fire escape and headed out of sight.

"You eager to go back inside?" Jade asked.

"Not really, but what choice do we have? Our team is in there. We have possible survivors as well."

"Hey, uh, Houston? We have a problem," Frank said over Chris's earpiece.

"What's wrong?" Chris asked.

"You know that barricade we set up earlier? Those things are tearing it apart. They'll be through shortly."

"How much time do you think you have?" Chris asked.

"I don't know. A couple minutes, maybe?"

"Okay. We have Officer Cohen getting some weapons for us, and we'll be on our way."

"Copy," Frank said.

"One thing after another, huh?" Jade said.

"You're not kidding," Chris replied.

He stepped to the edge of the rooftop to look below. An officer was heading towards the fire escape with a bag.

"Looks like someone is on their way up," Chris said.

Jade pointed to a building across the street.

"What's that?" she asked.

Chris squinted across the street. Something was on the roof of the building opposite of them.

No.

Not *something.*

Someone.

It looked as though they were sitting against the wall besides the door to the roof. It looked like they had something next to them. A laptop, maybe?

"That's a person," Chris said.

He looked to the fire escape and noticed Officer Cohen had returned to the roof. Chris pointed across the street to the person on the roof.

"Is that normal?" he asked the officer. "Someone sitting on the roof like that?"

Officer Cohen stepped closer to get a better look.

"Not usually. But maybe some people just go up there sometimes to get some privacy. Maybe to see what's going on over here?" he said.

"But at this time of night, you'd think it'd be empty, right?" Chris stated.

Officer Cohen was silent for a moment before he spoke. "I guess you're right."

"Can you send some officers to check it out? We're looking for the person who released the pathogen in this hotel. And someone sitting on the roof over there is a little suspicious," Chris said.

"Sure," Officer Cohen said. He reached for his walkie-talkie. "Flynn, come in."

There was static on the line before a voice said, "Flynn here."

"There's someone on the roof of the business center. Can you get a team and go up there and check it out?"

"On it," Flynn replied.

Officer Cohen turned to Chris and Jade and gave them a thumbs up.

"Thanks," Chris said.

He bent down to open the bag. It contained three handguns and about ten magazines.

Jade leaned in to look. "That's perfect."

Chris reached in, took the first handgun, and gave it to Jade, along with half of the magazines.

"Carry as much as you can," he told her. He then handed her the second gun, adding, "In case someone else needs it."

He took the third gun for himself and tucked the remaining magazines in his pockets.

"You're going back inside?" Officer Cohen asked.

"My team is in danger. We have survivors as well. One of them is a child. A group of infected are on their way to them now. They're tearing apart the barricade we had set up. We need to go help them."

"Then I'm coming too," Officer Cohen said.

"No. We don't know if the pathogen is still in the air. You could become infected. I'm not putting you in harm's way going back inside," Chris said. "You're staying here."

"No," he said, without hesitation. "You have survivors? A child? I want to help. I may be younger than you guys but I took an oath to serve and protect, and that's what I'm going to do. What kind of person would I be if I ignored the help you guys needed?"

"Look," Chris said, "I'm not going to ask you to come with us. This is *your* choice. It's dangerous inside and there's a possibility of becoming infected once you enter that hotel. I'm not going to say the extra hands wouldn't be helpful, because they would. But I just need you to know the risks before you make that decision."

Chris could see the officer's body trembling. But he could see the determination in his eyes. The officer wanted to be a hero. He wanted to serve his community and uphold the oath he had taken to safeguard the individuals he pledged to care for.

"I'm going with you," he said finally, his voice trembling.

"Then let's go," Chris said.

| 15 |

The banging grew louder and louder. The infected were getting close. Frank couldn't see the destruction in the hallway behind the closed door, but he knew the havoc those things were causing.

"What are we going to do?" Ellen asked, holding her daughter close.

Frank looked down at the few infected remaining in the lobby. He thought about taking them out one by one, but given the amount of ammo he had left, he didn't want to risk it. Especially if he had to use it to protect himself and everyone else up here on the second floor.

"We're going to hold our position for now," Frank said. "We can't go down without taking out the infected first."

"And why can't we kill them?" Emily asked.

"We have limited ammo."

"But what if they get through?" Emily said.

Frank raised his gun. "Then I'll shoot them. Plus, Chris and Jade are on their way back with another officer to help us."

"What if they don't make it in time?" Ellen said.

Frank swallowed hard. That thought hadn't crossed his mind. He had just assumed they'd arrive to help at any moment. Now he imagined a scenario where they didn't make it in time. Would he and the others survive? Would he be able to protect everyone?

"We'll be fine," he said confidently, even though he was far less confident than he had been.

The door rattled. The banging grew even louder.

"Hey, uh, Myles... how about joining us over here? We may need you any moment," Frank said.

Myles was kneeling beside the device, examining it. "Hold on," he told Frank.

"Holding on isn't something we can do right now, Myles."

"Sir, hold on one second," Myles said, before turning to Frank. "You need to do whatever you can for just a little longer. I'm on the phone with the company that designed this thing. They're walking me through how to debug it." He returned to examining the device, turning away from Frank.

Frank waved his hands. "Tell them to hurry the hell up. This is kind of an emergency."

Another loud bang came from the door.

Caroline screamed. Ellen was huddled in a corner with her daughter, far away from the door. Emily made her way to Frank and stood behind him.

"Don't let me die," she told him.

"I won't," Frank said. He aimed his handgun at the door.

The door rattled again. This time, the top hinge came loose, now dangling. The casing above the door broke apart and the door opened by a few inches. Fingers pushed through the cracks. The glass on the upper part of the door broke and hands were pushing through.

"They're getting through!" Ellen screamed.

"Myles! Hurry up!" Frank yelled.

The door continued to shake. The growling was directly outside the door. Arms started pushing through the opening.

Another crack on the door. The door began to split.

A head pushed through the side of the door. The infected looked at Frank and snarled at him. Spittle rained from its mouth.

Frank aimed his gun and fired a single shot to its head.

"Take that, you ugly son-of-a-bitch," he exclaimed.

He tapped on his ear. "Chris, how close are you? We're about to be overrun."

"Almost there," Chris replied. "Coming down the stairs now."

The door suddenly popped open and slammed onto the floor, knocking away the few pieces of furniture they had against it. A handful of infected fell on top of the door. Two stepped on the fallen ones in their rush towards Frank and Emily.

Frank aimed carefully and fired at the first infected, scoring a lethal headshot. He shifted his aim to the second, and fired. Another headshot and the second infected tumbled to the floor.

The remaining infected climbed to their feet. Frank took a quick glance, counting eight infected. Two more then darted into the room.

Frank took aim again and fired twice, taking both infected down.

The first infected rose to her feet. Her makeup had been smeared across her face. She headed towards Ellen and her daughter, Caroline. Frank swung his aim towards the infected and fired a shot.

He missed. The bullet whizzed past the monster's head by just an inch.

Frank fired again, and the infected swung sideways, and collapsed.

"Hey, Myles," he called. "A little help?"

Another infected stumbled into the room.

A thunderous growl filled the air. Before Frank and Emily could react, several infected began running towards them. Frank took out one of them before his gun clicked empty. He ejected the empty magazine rapidly and pushed in a new one.

He aimed.

The infected dropped from a gunshot to the head.

But Frank hadn't pulled the trigger. He looked past the horde of infected to the entrance and saw Jade in the doorway.

Thank God, he thought.

He aimed at another infected and pulled the trigger.

* * *

When Officer Cohen entered the room behind Jade, he was immediately taken back to his first fearful encounter with these monsters. They were swarming like a wild pack of predators, lunging at everyone in their path.

He aimed his weapon at the advancing infected, a woman wearing a blue dress stained with blood. He fired, hitting her in the chest. She slowed for a moment before continuing her march towards him, undeterred.

What the hell? he thought.

He shot her two more times, once in the shoulder and once in the stomach.

Again, she slowed for a moment, then continued towards Officer Cohen.

"Aim for the head. They go down quicker," he heard someone yell. It didn't matter who. He aimed higher, shot once and missed.

With an animalistic urge, the infected woman continued towards him. Her mouth opening in a loud and menacing snarl.

A chill ran down his spine. His hands shook. He couldn't control his aim. He fired again, and missed, having aimed too high. The infected woman kept coming.

Officer Cohen was startled to hear the screams he hadn't realized he was making. In a panic, he unloaded multiple shots in the direction of the infected woman. Luckily, one bullet struck her in the head. Her body lurched backwards before crumpling at the officer's feet. He leaped backwards in terror.

***

An infected dashed towards Myles, who was still kneeling on the ground toying with the device.

"Myles, look out!" Jade yelled.

Myles turned to find an infected bearing down on him. He spotted Jade aiming her weapon in his direction. Instinctively, he hit the floor and heard two gunshots ring out. A loud *thud* followed. Myles raised his head and looked into the eyes of a dead man lying next to him—an infected dead man. Myles backed away at the sight of him. He looked at Jade and gave her a single nod of appreciation.

Frank and Jade took out the final two infected.

"Clear?" Frank asked.

Jade surveyed the room and the hallway.

"Clear," she said.

"Where's Chris?" Frank asked.

"He's heading downstairs to prevent more from coming up here."

"How's he going to do that?" Frank asked.

***

Chris heard the gunshots and knew he only had seconds before the infected came knocking down the door on the first floor. He had dragged the ladder down the stairs with him, hoping to use it as a giant door stopper. Luckily for him, his idea worked. The ladder was just long enough that he had the legs planted against the wall and the top of the ladder against the door. He hoped it was good enough to hold.

He started to head back to the second floor, but stopped when the door started to shake.

There they are, he thought.

He watched as the relentless thuds from behind the door achieved nothing. The plan had been successful, and the door wasn't budging. He was safe—for now.

Chris smiled. Finally, something had gone right.

He jogged back upstairs to join the rest of the team.

| 16 |

The second floor was a mess. The barricade was decimated with broken furniture everywhere. Dead bodies covered in blood filled the lounge area in which they were taking shelter.

Jade stood over Ellen and her daughter, making sure they were okay. Frank, Officer Cohen, and Emily were together by the balcony, watching the few infected wander around below them. Myles was still kneeling on the floor with the device.

Chris entered the room.

"Jesus Christ, what happened in here?"

Everyone turned to see him stepping over the deceased infected.

"You're all lucky I'm not one of those things," Chris said. "I could have come behind any of you and taken you out. Who's watching the door?"

Frank stepped away from the balcony. "I got it."

As he made his way to the door, Chris walked past him and took up residence where Frank had been standing.

"How are you holding up?" he asked the young officer.

"I kinda freaked out during the firefight earlier, but I'm still here," Officer Cohen replied.

"Good." Chris patted him on the back. "How about you?" he asked Emily, leaning past Officer Cohen to see her.

"I'm alright. I'll be better when I'm out of here."

Chris nodded. "We all will. Hang in there."

He noticed Myles fumbling with the top part of his hazmat suit.

"Myles, what are you doing?" Chris asked.

Myles disconnected the head portion of his suit and removed it. He placed it on the floor and took a deep breath.

"That feels so much better," he said.

"Are we good?" Chris asked him.

Myles nodded. "Yeah, we're good. No pathogen detected. We're safe."

"Thank God," Officer Cohen said.

Frank began ripping off the head portion of his hazmat suit as well. "If that's the case," he said, struggling, "I'm taking this thing off too."

Jade begun taking hers off as well.

"What about us?" Ellen said, starting to stand up.

"I don't know yet," Chris said. "You were inside the hotel when the virus was released, but it hasn't affected you. So I think we need to get some tests done on you guys to make sure you're okay. You made it this far without anything happening. So that's something to feel confident about."

Ellen picked up her daughter and held her in her arms, swaying gently.

"Now what, boss?" Frank asked.

Chris looked at Frank and then at Officer Cohen. "Now that we know it's safe, we need to get your guys in here to help us clear out anyone left in this hotel and get the survivors out of here. We'll go room by room if we have to."

"I'll make the call," the officer said. He grabbed his walkie-talkie and held down the button. "Flynn, come in."

"Flynn here, go ahead," the voice replied.

"We're safe over here. No virus in the air. We can enter the building. Can you prepare to send in the team?" Officer Cohen said.

"Yeah. I'll radio over to the officers in a minute. I'm actually just making my way inside the office building now. Heading to the elevator," Flynn said.

"Okay. Any update on the roof issue?" Officer Cohen said.

Frank tilted his head, confused. "What roof issue?"

"We saw something on the roof across the street," Chris said. He pointed to the officer. "He sent some officers over to check it out."

"I'll let you know when I get up there," Flynn said over the walkie-talkie.

"Tell him I'm going back to the roof to monitor from this side of the street," Chris said.

Officer Cohen passed along Chris's plans to Flynn before ending the conversation.

"Okay everyone, here's the plan," Chris said. "I'm heading back to the roof to monitor what's going on across the street. Officer Cohen will be joining me." He turned to face Jade. "I'm leaving you in charge here. Once the officers come in and you guys secure the lobby, get a team of medics to assist Ellen, her daughter, and Emily. Got it?"

"Yes, sir," she said.

"Frank, you and Myles assist the officers coming in."

Chris paused for a moment, remembering Stevens' wishes—not killing the infected. He believed there may be hope for them. Now that they had control of the situation, maybe there was something they could do.

"Let's take a different approach," Chris said. "Contain the infected, don't kill them. Stevens had an idea that there may be a chance to reverse the effects of the virus by studying it."

"You want us to do *what?*" Frank asked.

"You heard me. Contain. Do not kill unless your life is in immediate danger. We don't know anything about this virus. There may be a way to save these people. We'll have a larger team now, we can handle it. Understood?"

"Understood," Frank replied.

"Good. Open communication everyone. Final stretch. Let's get out of here quickly and safely," Chris said.

| 17 |

Chris and Officer Cohen parted ways with the team and headed for the roof, sprinting up a seemingly endless stairwell. Horrific evidence of destruction surrounded them—gaping bullet holes in walls and doors, broken furniture scattered about, stained carpets caked with dried blood. Chris imagined the crew responsible for the cleanup once they had completed their mission.

Will they even repair this place? he thought. *It's full of death, and tainted memories. Maybe they'll just knock it down and start over.*

They stepped over a few dead infected on their way to the roof, then stepped outside.

"You think this is over?" Officer Cohen asked.

"I sure hope so," Chris said.

At the fire escape, Chris looked down to see the group of officers entering the building. He was eager to end this. There had been too much loss and bloodshed.

"Hey," Officer Cohen said, "there's Flynn." He pointed across the street at the office building. Flynn had just stepped onto the roof.

A light suddenly beamed from his hand.

He walked around, checking his surroundings with the flashlight. Whatever Chris had seen earlier wasn't there anymore.

"You see anything?" Officer Cohen asked, speaking into his walkie-talkie.

Flynn stopped moving and responded. "No, nothing here."

"Is he by himself?" Chris asked.

Officer Cohen shrugged. "Flynn, are you by yourself?"

"Yeah, why?"

"Dammit. I asked you to send a group of officers. We're looking for the man behind the attack, and he might be in there," Chris said.

"I got it. Don't worry about it," Flynn responded.

Chris took a step away from Officer Cohen and shook his head.

"Did you see anyone on your way up there?" Officer Cohen asked.

"No." Flynn shined his flashlight around again. "There's nothing here. If someone was up here, they—"

A flash went off near the officer. A popping noise echoed in the distance.

Flynn fell and the flashlight rolled away from him.

Now another shadowy figure stood in his place.

"Flynn! Come in!" Officer Cohen yelled into the walkie-talkie.

There was no response.

"Flynn!" Officer Cohen yelled again.

"He's dead," Chris said. "I told you. A team should have gone in."

Chris grabbed the ladder and begun heading down.

"Hello there," a voice said through the walkie-talkie.

Chris paused in response to the familiar voice coming from the officer's walkie-talkie. He climbed back to the roof and snatched it from Officer Cohen.

"Who is this?" he asked, staring across the rooftops at the mysterious figure.

"I believe you refer to me as the Doctor."

"Why are you doing this?"

"Why not?"

"What do you mean, 'why not?' You enjoy killing people?"

"No, I *do not* enjoy killing people. I enjoy life. I enjoy creating viruses and giving *them* life. If the life I create ends up hurting or killing others, so be it."

"You murdered possibly hundreds of people with the virus you released inside this hotel."

"No, *I* didn't murder anyone. The virus did."

"You created it," Chris snapped.

"That's like saying gun manufacturers kill people with the guns they create instead of the people who use them," the Doctor said.

"But in this analogy, you created the gun *and* pulled the trigger."

"Touché, Mr. Hoffman. You deserve more credit than I give you."

He said my name. Does he know me?

"You know my name."

"I do, and your whole team—Jade Burleigh, Frank Parker, and Myles Johnson. I should probably get to know the people who are trying to hunt me down, right?"

"What do you want?" Chris asked.

"What I really want is to know is how those super-powered freaks do what they do—and I may know soon. Mind control was about the best I could have done with my limited time and resources."

Was he talking about the incidents in Decker City surrounding the guy who could move things without touching them?

The Doctor continued. "But I'll take what I have instead—the power to create killers of anyone. It was fun to watch the virus take over, and extremely entertaining watching you guys try to take them down. What did you guys call them—infected?"

"You're not getting away with this," Chris said.

"But I already have. Look, Chris, it's been fun catching up. But I need to get going. I've got an escape to attend to."

Chris was about to respond, until he saw the silhouette in the distance disappear through the door on the roof.

Chris tossed the walkie-talkie back to Officer Cohen. "Get a group of officers to surround that building now. I don't want anyone getting out of there."

He began sliding down the ladder, making his way to the ground.

He was going after the Doctor.

| 18 |

"The Doctor is here," Chris said, pressing on his earpiece. "He's across the street in the office building. I'm in pursuit."

He slid down the ladder and set off down the first flight of steps.

"Wait, how?" Jade asked.

"He was here the whole time. He said something about watching us."

"Watching us?' Myles said. "Maybe he had access to the hotel security cameras."

"Do you need our help?" Frank said.

"Yes, but we need to get those survivors out and make sure that the hotel is contained first. I have a few guys surrounding the building the Doctor is in," Chris replied. "Make sure everyone is safe, and that place is secured. Then get your asses over here. We need to find this guy."

Chris jumped off the staircase to the ground, then sprinted across the street towards the main entrance of the office building. Officer Cohen trailed not far behind.

Two officers standing at the entrance met Chris as he approached.

"Has anyone come in or out of here?" Chris asked as he pulled on the handle of the glass door.

Both officers shook their head.

"All the doors are locked," one said. "No one has entered the building. Are you sure someone is in there?"

Chris ignored his question and pulled out his gun. He aimed it at the glass door and fired two shots, shattering it.

"Hey!" the officers yelled, stepping backwards.

Chris turned to look at one of the officers. "Watch the door."

"You can't just do that!" the officer responded.

Chris disregarded him and stepped over the shattered glass, which crunched under his shoes as he made his way inside.

Officer Cohen approached the two officers and apologized for Chris's tactics, then followed him inside.

The lights flickered to life as Chris surveyed the lobby with a keen eye. The elevators were at the center of the lobby. To one side was an impressive corner office encased in decorative glass walls. To his other side was a hallway leading to a staircase.

"There," he said, pointing.

"The stairs?" Officer Cohen asked.

"Yeah. The two officers outside will see anyone coming out of the elevators." Chris began jogging along the hall. "Plus, I don't think the Doctor would be stupid enough to take the elevator."

"Why?"

"Too confined. He'd be trapping himself inside a box."

Chris opened the door and aimed his weapon into the dark staircase. A second later, the lights flickered on.

Motion detector.

He looked up the stairs, moving his weapon in the direction of his vision.

Empty.

"Let's go," he said.

The two of them started climbing the stairs. Chris led the way, taking the stairs slowly and constantly checking the corners above him.

Officer Cohen stopped at the door to the second floor.

"You don't want to check here first?"

Chris kept moving upwards. "No. Top down. He was up on the roof. My guess is he's up high."

Officer Cohen started following Chris. "But if he wanted to escape, wouldn't he want to be closer to the ground? Easier exit."

"True. And I think that's what he'd want you to think. I think he's on one of the top floors. Maybe in the room from which he watched us. He knew we'd be on him quickly. He'd have more time to get ready for us or hide if he stayed on a higher floor rather than going to a lower one."

"I hope you're right," Officer Cohen said.

"I am," Chris said confidently.

As Chris and Officer Cohen climbed the five flights of stairs all the way to the top floor, Chris noticed blood on the staircase above. There were droplets on the stairs, leading beyond the door.

"You think he's hurt?" Officer Cohen asked.

"I don't know," Chris said. He cracked the door open and scanned the hallway.

As he stepped out the door, a gunshot echoed around the hallway. Instinctively, he ducked and retreated to safety.

Another shot came. It sounded as though it hit the wall outside the door.

More bullets came whizzing in Chris's direction.

He stuck his gun through the door and blindly fired three shots down the hallway.

He heard a window shatter in the distance.

The Doctor returned fire. Chris remained in the stairwell as he shot towards him.

He pointed to Officer Cohen. "Take my position. After he's done firing, return fire. I'm going to make my way into the hallway and try to get a better shot."

Officer Cohen nodded and moved up the stairs.

The hallway was quiet now. The Doctor had stopped shooting.

"Now," Chris said.

Officer Cohen moved from around the door and released a slew of bullets towards the Doctor.

Knowing he had to move quickly, Chris jumped from cover and pushed himself against the opposing wall. He raised his weapon in preparation for any movement from the Doctor. He crept forward, closer and closer to the corner behind which the Doctor was hiding.

The carpeted floor silenced his steps as he crept up on the Doctor. The glass surrounding the conference room at the end of the hallway was shattered. The white walls were left riddled with jagged, gaping holes as a result of the countless bullets. Not only had Chris and his team destroyed the hotel across the street, but now he had begun to destroy the fifth floor of this office building.

Officer Cohen stopped shooting.

The Doctor peeked out from cover and fired a single shot. Chris fired back, and the Doctor retreated instantly.

"Keep firing!" Chris shouted to Officer Cohen.

The officer continued to return fire as Chris made his way along the hall, staying close to the wall, gun aimed. With every step, he expected the Doctor to return fire—but he was ready. He was prepared to kill the Doctor if he had to. He'd prefer to arrest him and interrogate him. Lock him up and throw away the key. But he'd certainly defend himself if the Doctor dared to shoot at him.

Officer Cohen stopped shooting. Chris rushed to the corner, anticipating finding the Doctor hiding there.

He wasn't.

Chris scanned the area and noticed blood on the ground. In his peripheral vision, he saw more blood on the wall.

Did I hit him? he thought.

"Cohen, on me!" Chris yelled.

As the officer joined Chris, he saw the blood too.

"He's hurt," he said.

He aimed his weapon along the hallway. "Let's go."

The two of them held their guns forward and slowly advanced down the hallway.

"Chris, come in," Jade said over their communication devices.

"Go ahead," he said, not taking his eyes off the hallway in front of him.

"The survivors are safe with the medics," Jade said. "We had to take out a few of the infected, but we were able to confine a few of them to a room. Frank, Myles and I are on our way over. What's your location?"

"Fifth floor. He's here. Possibly injured. Send whoever you can," Chris said.

"Copy. On our way."

Chris clenched his gun. He felt he might pull the trigger at any moment. But he wanted to catch this guy, not kill him. Chris took his next step cautiously, trying to push away the nervousness.

He saw another drop of blood on the carpet, then another not far beyond it.

Chris moved onwards, scanning the area for the next trace of blood the Doctor had left behind. Then he saw it. To his immediate left was a door with a smeared, bloodied handprint on it.

He pointed to the door, then examined it. A light shone through a gap alongside it.

Is this a trap? he thought.

He didn't care. He didn't want to waste anymore time. If the Doctor was in there, he wanted to get him *now.*

Chris placed his palm on the door and slowly pushed it open. If it was a trap, the squeaky door would have given them away.

But nothing happened.

Chris slipped through the door and walked through the small hallway before finding himself in a small, private office. To his right was an empty desk with a shelving unit above it. Directly in front of him was a table with three monitors on it.

In front of the table was a chair, and in the chair sat the Doctor.

He faced computer monitors with his back to Chris and Officer Cohen. The Doctor had on his white lab coat. His right hand hung from the side of the armrest, holding a gun.

Chris aimed at the chair. "Drop the gun!" he commanded.

The Doctor didn't move. He didn't drop the gun. He said nothing.

Chris took a step closer. "I said, d*rop the gun!*" His voice was much more harsh and threatening than before.

What the hell is his problem? he thought. *Why isn't he listening?*

He took another few steps forward and kicked the Doctor's gun out of his hand, then yanked his shoulder and spun the chair around.

The man in the lab coat didn't move.

Was he dead?

The Doctor's eyes were shut. Chris poked him with his gun, looking for signs of life. The Doctor still didn't move.

This man was dead.

Chris reached to check his pulse at his neck.

"Flynn?" Officer Cohen said.

"What?" Chris asked, retracting his hand sharply.

"Oh my God. That's Flynn."

Chris pointed at the man in the chair. "Him?"

"Yes. Why is he dressed like that?"

The man in the chair wore the Doctor's white lab coat. Underneath was a plain white shirt, and light blue doctor scrubs to complete the ensemble.

"He took his uniform," Chris said. "Call your team and let them know." He placed his finger to his ear, communicating with his team. "The Doctor is wearing a police uniform. I repeat, he's in a police uniform. Check the ID of every officer."

Chris stiffened with anger. He realized his jaw was clenched. He opened his mouth to breathe to release the tension in his face.

How did he get past me?

He started to put the puzzle together. The blood outside must have been Flynn's—a way to lure him.

The Doctor must have pretended to be injured and used the blood to get us in here. He had this planned before we even got up here. There is no way he had done this within seconds of us shooting at him. He was a step ahead.

And he's slowing me down.

"Dammit," Chris said. He rushed past Officer Cohen, out of the room, and towards the elevators. He hit the call button, then looked up at the display to see that the elevators were on the bottom floor. The numbers flashed as the elevator begun its ascent.

A moment later, the elevator dinged, and the doors opened.

Chris rushed in and continuously hammered the lobby button until the doors closed. He waited as the numbers blinked one by one as he moved past each floor.

He trembled with rage, feeling as if his heart was pounding out of his chest. He thought he had the Doctor cornered, only to realize he had been outsmarted. Chris was terrified of what might happen if he failed to catch him.

The elevator dinged, and the door opened—too slowly. Chris pushed it open to step off the elevator quicker.

Two officers stood by the elevator—the same two who had stood by the front door earlier.

"You again?" the officer on the right said.

Chris ignored the comment. "Did someone come off the elevator recently? Maybe a minute or two ago?"

"Yeah. He said he was getting something from his vehicle outside," the officer replied.

"You let him go?" Chris furiously asked.

"We didn't know we had to stop him. We got the call about that after he left the building."

"Did you go after him, then?"

"I looked outside, but I didn't see him. Figured he'd come back any minute."

"And did he come back?"

The two officers looked at each other in confusion.

"No."

As angry as Chris was, he didn't have time to keep speaking to these idiots. He stormed past them and made his way outside. He stood at the entrance to the building, scanning the streets. A group of four officers stood by a police vehicle in the street, and another two were walking side by side to the right.

Chris darted out into the street. Both directions were barricaded with combinations of cars, police tape, and cones. Onlookers stood behind the cordon, watching the chaotic scene unfold. A few people held up cell phones, taking pictures or recording the events taking place.

Flashing lights lit up the night sky, reflecting from the windows of the surrounding buildings. The light drew Chris's attention back to the hotel.

All the death and destruction that happened inside that building. The loss of a friend. The families of those who had been destroyed by a horrific virus unleashed by a terrorist.

He had let this terrorist, the Doctor, get away—again. He wasn't this close to catching him the first time, though. This time, he almost had him. He knew where he was. At one point, the Doctor had been right in front of him.

And he had escaped.

Chris stood in the street, looking for anything to give him hope of finding this criminal.

He found nothing.

The Doctor had escaped.

| 19 |

Chris, Jade, Frank, and Myles returned to their headquarters to investigate the incident further. They had taken the few pieces of equipment left behind by the Doctor in the room where Chris had found Flynn, the deceased officer.

Myles had also managed to make copies of the security camera feeds of the hotel and the business complex, so they could see the Doctor's movements.

Myles pointed to the computer screen in front of him and Chris. "There he is."

"And he just walked right out of the building. No one even stopped him," Chris said.

"What did you expect?" Jade said. "He was in a police uniform. He blended right in."

Chris shook his head. "Myles, where did he go after he left the building?"

Myles tapped at the keyboard, and another screen popped up. "Here," he said, pointing to the screen. "He walked down the alley." Myles tapped another key, bringing up a different viewpoint. "He comes into view here and then walks right up to that red car."

"Do we have a license plate?" Chris asked.

"It won't matter," Myles said. "Just watch."

As the Doctor approached the car, he pulled something from his pocket—presumably a key fob. He pointed it at the trunk, which popped open. He pulled something out along with a rectangular object.

"What's he doing?" Frank asked.

"Just watch," Myles said.

The Doctor closed the trunk and placed the rectangular object on it. He leaned over and started doing something to the license plate.

Chris nodded. "He's changing his license plate."

"Yeah," Myles said.

"I'm assuming you already looked up the numbers from both plates."

Myles nodded.

"Fake?" Jade asked.

Myles nodded again. "No record comes up from a search on either of them."

"Can we use traffic cameras to see where he went?" Frank asked.

"I'm working with the Department of Transportation," Myles replied. "We only know that he went north. But other than that, we don't have much else to go on."

"So, we're back to square one," Chris said.

The room was silent.

This wasn't what any of them had expected.

A text alert broke the uncomfortable silence. The team members all reached for their phones.

It was Frank's phone that had made the sound. He stared at it in silence.

"Your girlfriend, *Emily*?" Jade asked, smirking.

He sent a message and placed the phone on the table. "Not my girlfriend. I texted her asking how she was feeling and she responded."

"And when have we ever made friends and texted with people we met in the field?" Jade replied.

"I was being a concerned individual."

"Yeah? How are Ellen and her daughter? You text them too?"

Frank rolled his eyes.

"Shut up," he said.

"Aww, Frank has a crush," Myles said. "And he's blushing."

Jade started laughing, which made Myles laugh as well.

The friendly banter lightened the mood.

Chris had overheard them, but he ignored them as he continued to process what had just happened.

His phone went off. He snatched it up—it was a text from his boss.

New mission incoming. My office tomorrow @ 08:00. You'll receive the details when you get here.

Chris had to do what he could to put this mission behind him, for now. He had to think of the positives that had come from it: They had rescued survivors, eliminated the majority of the infected, prevented any more from escaping, and had secured a few of them for testing—per Stevens' wishes.

He'd find the Doctor again. He knew they'd cross paths. Maybe this next mission would put him on that path. Maybe the one after that. He didn't know. But he had a job to do, and tomorrow he'd find out what that job would be. Until then, he'd continue looking for anything to bring him closer to finding the Doctor.

Confirmed, Chris texted back.

He looked up at the team, who were all laughing together. He smiled and joined in on the roasting of Frank.

Epilogue

The Doctor sat in his car at a rest stop off the highway. He reclined his seat slightly and ate the rest of the chicken sandwich he had bought from the convenience store.

When he finished eating, he removed his stolen police uniform and changed into sweatpants and a T-shirt. Changing in the car was a little difficult, but he didn't want to change inside the convenience store restroom. Too many eyes. Maybe people wondering why he was changing out of a police uniform.

He folded his newly acquired police uniform neatly and placed it on the seat next to him.

This may come in handy, he thought.

His phone dinged.

He took it from the cup holder.

I have the blood sample.

The Doctor smiled. He texted back, *Let's meet.*

His heart fluttered. Something tingling in his stomach. Was he excited?

This was what he had been waiting for. He was finally going to analyze the blood of someone with super-powers.

His phone dinged again.

Leaving Mapleton now. What's your location?

The Doctor texted back.

Bloomsville.

At first there was no response. He kept staring at his phone, wondering if something had happened.

There's an abandoned building on Kingsbury Street. Meet in two hours.

The Doctor responded by sending a thumbs up emoji.

He felt jittery. Excitement flowed through him like a child on Christmas morning. There was a gift waiting for him. He couldn't wait to unwrap it and see what was inside. He suddenly had a rush of energy.

The Doctor was eager to get started on his next project—working on the blood from someone with super-powers.

Oh, the possibilities, he thought.

He rubbed his hands together and smiled.

Once he had collected himself, he returned his seat to an upright position and started the car.

ABOUT THE AUTHOR

Justin Richman has had a fascination with superheroes and science fiction since he was a child. He has memorabilia from both the DC and Marvel universe all over his home office which help give him inspiration to write. He lives in Pennsylvania with his two sons. Currently, Justin is writing the third book in his superhero series, The Defenders Saga.

You can also find him frequently posting about bizarre stories on Facebook @jrichmanauthor. 'Like' his page on Facebook and Instagram so you can follow his exciting posts and to keep up with his future projects.

Make sure to visit his website & subscribe to his newsletter at www.justinrichman.com to be the first to know about his upcoming stories!